RESCUE DOGS

DOGS

GEM

RESCUE DOGS

GEM

JANE B. MASON
AND SARAH HINES STEPHENS

Scholastic Inc.

ISBN 978-1-338-36213-8

10 9 8 7 6 5 4 3 2 1   21 22 23 24 25

Printed in the U.S.A. 40
First printing 2021

Book design by Stephanie Yang

For the dogs who rescue people
and the people who rescue dogs

01

The morning started out like it always did. Gem woke up on Lexa's bed, like she always did. Lexa's mom yelled about how many times she'd told her daughter, "No dogs on the furniture," like she always did. Gem hopped down from her cozy spot, ears low, and slunk toward the door so she wouldn't have to hear the shouting. That was when things got weird and different. There was no more shouting. Lexa didn't object to the rule. The mom stepped out of Gem's way with a sigh and mumbled something Gem didn't understand.

Things got even stranger after that. The

always-hungry young puppy had barely swallowed her last bite of breakfast when Lexa's brother, Jay, clicked her leash onto her collar. He dropped down to one knee and pushed his face into her reddish-gold fur. That wasn't something he usually did. Then the skinny boy stood up, sniffed, and pulled the retriever outside, toward the car.

The whole family piled into the minivan: the mom, the dad, Lexa, and Jay. Usually when they were all together on an outing, there was a lot of talking and yelling or singing along to loud music—and the car was loaded with food. Today it was quiet. Lexa didn't even reach up front to turn on the radio. She just slumped in her seat, not saying anything.

When the car stopped and the people got out, Gem watched the family through the window of the car. Their faces hung low. She wagged to try and cheer them up, and also to ask if they were going to let her out. Jay opened the back door, but none of them looked her in the eye. And there was no trail or picnic spot waiting . . . just a big parking lot and a low square building.

"We just can't keep her anymore," the mom said, breaking the silence to answer a question nobody had asked.

Jay and Lexa walked on either side of Gem. They led her through a swinging door and into a room with hard floors and hard chairs. It smelled of dogs and dogs and dogs . . . and sadness. And fear. The smell made Gem a little afraid, too. She whimpered and felt Lexa's hand in her fur.

A woman greeted them from behind a desk. She talked to the mom and dad, and they passed papers back and forth. Nobody smiled. After the woman put the papers on a board, she opened a door that led into another, bigger room. She was still talking, but now Gem couldn't hear her words over the barking. Dozens of dogs behind metal fences lined the walls of the big room. The barks echoed. Some were scared barks. Some were warning barks. Some were begging barks. The desperate noises made Gem's floppy ears ache. They twitched forward, but she couldn't block out the sounds. She looked at Lexa, then at Jay, to ask what was happening. She didn't understand. What were they doing here? This was not a fun place. She wanted to go home.

Neither of the children could look at the young golden retriever. They could barely move. The dad took the leash from Jay's hand and pulled Gem behind the woman, who was leading them down the cement path between the rows of chain-link kennels. The woman walked briskly. She smelled like the disinfectant spray the mom used when Gem had accidents in the house. She opened the door of an empty kennel. She patted the metal, making it clang. "In here," she instructed. "Then say your goodbyes. It's best to do it quickly."

Lexa swallowed so hard Gem heard it while the dad directed her toward the cage.

Gem slunk through the door, confused and sad and worried.

"I'm so sorry, kids," the mom said, covering her mouth with her hand. "It's just too much."

Gem didn't know what the mom was saying exactly. But the sound and smell of her gave the sensitive pup a lot of clues. Gem could smell sorrow, like a rotten apple. And briny guilt. And she thought maybe she smelled something else, too . . . sickly-sweet confusion.

"Woof!" She let out a short sharp bark—a question—to ask what was going on. Lexa stepped closer, reaching for Gem.

The disinfectant woman snorted impatiently and swung the gate closed. Shutting Gem in, shutting the kids out.

Gem looked at her family on the other side of the fence, her ears and tail low. The mom wouldn't meet her eyes. "The digging . . . the endless digging," she said to no one in particular. The barking of the other dogs quieted enough for Gem to hear a word she knew: "dig." Her tail drooped lower. She remembered the yelling after she dug up the roses.

And the flower bed. And the earth underneath the porch steps. The mom had yelled and called her a bad dog. Bad dog. Gem knew those words, too. And she didn't like them.

Suddenly, Gem knew why she was there, in a kennel. She knew why her family wouldn't look at her. It was because she was a bad dog. Because of the digging. And the accidents.

Gem let out a whimper.

Jay started to cry. The dad put his arm around him. He reached for Lexa, too, but she shook him off. She knelt down and looked at Gem through the fence. Her eyes were extra wet and sparkly. Jay's shoulders shuddered with silent sobs, but Lexa blinked back tears. She was working hard to hold it together. Gem could smell her determination.

The young dog's snout felt full of sadness and regret, her family's and her own. The regret gnawed at her. She hadn't really wanted to dig up everything in the backyard. It was . . . just . . . so . . . lonely at the house when the family was gone. All day. Every day. And there were *so many smells* in the soil! The smells wafted into her nose. They called to her. They made her paws itch to uncover them. Gem felt sure if she dug deep enough or in just the right spot, she would find . . . something . . .

"Do you promise she'll get a new home?" Lexa choked out, looking at the disinfectant lady. She pressed her hand to the chain link. Gem whined and licked her palm through the metal mesh.

"We do everything we can to make sure *every* animal finds a home," the woman answered. She was tapping her foot impatiently and jotting things down on a clipboard . . . things about Gem.

"What are you writing?" Jay shrugged out from under his dad's arm, stepping closer to the woman and looking at her defiantly. "What are you saying about our dog?" He reached for the clipboard. The woman stepped back with a tired sigh, and the dad put his hand on Jay's shoulder to stop him.

"It's okay, Jay. She wants to help. Everyone here does. And she's not *our* dog anymore."

Gem saw Lexa's eyes flash. "Do you have to write about the digging?" she asked.

The woman pressed her lips into a straight line. "We have to be honest about an animal's behavior. If we aren't, it can lead to a bad fit and the dog will end up right back here again."

Lexa looked from her mom to her dad and back to her mom. A whine crept into her voice. "You can't do this! Gem is part of our family! Would you send me away if I messed up the yard?" Her voice cracked, and she shook the fencing, which rattled.

Gem whined, too. She stopped licking and started to pace. She wanted to get out of this cage. To jump on Lexa and make her laugh.

"We've been over this. Let's just go home," the mom said softly. "Please."

Gem barked again. Yes. Home. She wanted to go home, too!

Letting another puff of air out her nose, the disinfectant lady nodded.

The dad bent over and unwrapped Lexa's fingers from the chain link. He tried to hold her hand, but Lexa yanked it away.

The tears finally spilled out of Lexa's eyes and down her cheeks. "Bye, Gem," she whispered. Then she turned.

Gem watched helplessly, whining and pacing, jumping up to put her front feet on the metal fencing as her family walked away. When they disappeared through the door, she dropped back to all fours and began to scratch at the concrete at the bottom of the gate. Her nails clicked uselessly against the hard surface over and over. Finally she sat down on the cold concrete and let out a long, mournful howl.

02

"Ooowwwooooo!" Gem's desolate howl echoed in the big room, and after several long moments, other dogs joined the discarded retriever's sorrowful song.

The mournful music brought the disinfectant lady back. She poked her head in the door, and though her brow was creased, her eyes looked softer now. She walked over to Gem's kennel and shook her head. "Did you start this racket?" she asked. "I don't know many howling golden retrievers . . ." She blinked and took a deep breath, letting it all out in a silent howl of her own, and then went back to her office work.

The howling continued for a full fifteen minutes. Then, after the rest of the dogs had worn out or given up, Gem kept going. The final wail left her throat at last, and with it her last hope of her family's return. They were not coming back for her. They were not her family anymore. The empty feeling she sometimes had in the backyard on long lonely days sat in her chest like a hole, and her paws began to move with a life of their own. While the other shelter dogs curled onto their beds, she dug at the floor. She dug and dug and dug.

Gem dug until her nails were broken and bloody. She didn't know what else to do. Her family. Her kids. Her life. They were all gone. She was all that was left. Alone.

🐾 🐾 🐾

Sometime during the first horrible day at the shelter, a worker brought Gem a bowl of food and fresh water. The next morning, both were still in her cage, untouched.

"Oh! You haven't eaten? You poor pup!" a

gentle voice crooned. It was Edna, one of the shelter volunteers.

Gem thumped her tail at the sound of the kind voice, momentarily forgetting where she was. Then it all came back. She tried to stand and whimpered. Her paws were tender from clawing at the unforgiving surfaces. She lay down to lick away the dried blood around her nails. Everything hurt!

"Oh no. Look at that." Edna crouched down to get a closer look. "What did you do to yourself?"

The short, white-haired woman stroked Gem's soft rosy-golden fur. It wasn't unusual to see sensitive dogs nervously lick themselves bald in patches or chew away their own skin with sadness and worry. She wasn't sure how this dog had managed to injure her paws so badly, but she was pretty sure she knew why: The poor pup was anxious and depressed. After gathering some supplies to help treat Gem's injured paws, she spotted the scratches on the concrete by the gate.

Gem felt herself relax a little as she listened to

Edna's soft voice. She didn't want her feet to be touched, but the woman was gentle as she trimmed the torn nails and put ointment and bandages on her broken skin.

"No licking!" Edna scolded kindly. "And no taking these off."

Holding one of her front paws aloft, Gem shook it gingerly. She hated the bandages, but she was too sad and tired to chew them loose.

Edna stood up. She volunteered twice a week at the animal shelter because she couldn't have a pet of her own. She loved the work and spending time with the animals—especially the dogs—who required extra attention. But there were so many animals! She needed to continue her rounds, feeding and walking the rest of the pups waiting to be found or adopted. She closed the gate and looked back. There was something about forlorn Gem that made her linger.

Curious, Edna took the clipboard off the hook on Gem's kennel. Every dog had a list of notes—useful information for people looking to adopt, as well as the dog's more challenging characteristics. Did she bark too much? Did he chew too much? Or dislike children? Gem's reddish fur, floppy ears, sweet brown nose, and soulful eyes made her a great candidate for adoption. The sheet clipped to the board said she was great with kids, and Edna knew that the breed was notorious for loving people—usually preferring human company to that of other dogs—so she wondered what her undesirable traits might be. The more she read, the more her concern rose. With a single nod, she replaced the clipboard. Gem was a digger. And if the damage she had done to herself was any indication, she was also extra sensitive, anxious, a little obsessive, and did not like to be left alone.

"Things are going to get better, sweet girl," Edna said as she opened the kennel door. She could spare a few more minutes. She sighed, wishing she felt as certain as she sounded. It would take time—possibly weeks—for Gem's paws to heal, and she wouldn't be placed on the adoptable list until they did. Those weeks were going to be tough on a dog as perceptive and tender as this one. Edna sat and gave Gem another long pet, lingering behind her ears when the pup leaned into her touch. The paws would heal in time, Edna knew. She just wasn't so sure about the dog's broken heart.

03

Though there was no cushy couch (or Lexa to cuddle with, or Jay to tussle with, or scraps slipped under the table from the dad's plate, or a yard to dig in), there was a rhythm to life in the shelter that Gem settled into. She did not wag much—only for Edna—but she didn't howl or claw at the floors anymore, either. Her paws had healed. She had food and water. She had a tidy kennel and a dry dog bed to sleep on, and it helped to hear the breathing (and snoring!) of the other dogs at night. Gem was not alone. Still, she was very lonely.

The best days were the days when Edna came. Gem loved the soft, round woman who'd made her paws better. She was gentle, smelled like cinnamon, and never raised her voice. She also kept treats in her pockets and made sure she spent extra time with Gem, scratching her in the good spot behind her ears before she left. Sometimes, Edna took Gem out for a walk by herself, without any other dogs. When it was just the two of them, Edna led her to a spot behind the shrubs where the dogs all ran and peed. She showed her an expanse of dirt without any grass or flowers and kicked at it with her comfortable shoes to release some of the smells in the rich soil.

"It's okay to dig here," Edna said. Gem scratched cautiously and looked back at Edna to make sure she was still smiling. "Go on!" the woman encouraged her. Gem scratched again, and then with both paws she slowly began to dig. The smells crowded into her snout, and she held them in, letting them swirl around behind her nostrils. Holding scents in like this was almost like tasting them. Rotting wood! Insects! Rainwater! Mushrooms! Gem's feet flew, faster and faster, paw over paw, spraying dirt and unearthing aromas. She dug deeper and deeper, digging down and down to . . . where?

Gem paused and shook the dirt from her fur. Where was she trying to dig to? What was she digging for? She wasn't sure. She only knew that she *needed* to dig. It filled a hole inside her, if only for a moment . . . a hole that had been there for as long as she could remember.

Watching Gem dig, Edna felt a small, sad empty spot in her own chest. The poor pup looked happy as she sent the soil flying, but she also looked a little desperate, as if she were frantically searching for something. Edna bit her thumbnail, which was already short from habit and worry. A dog this smart needed the right person to help her feel stable—someone steady and calm. Edna was determined to help her find that certain someone.

When Richard came into the shelter a few days

later, Edna zeroed in on him as a candidate for Gem right away. He was calm and laid-back, and when Edna asked him why he wanted a dog his answer was spot-on: "I need company. I guess I'm looking for a new best friend." Darlene, the director at the shelter, who Edna was pretty sure took baths in Lysol, was steering him toward a terrier mix—a lapdog—when Edna interrupted.

"You seem like more of a 'big dog' guy," she said. Really, what she was thinking was that he seemed like a worn-in easy chair in human form. He didn't look capable of raising his voice, and his eyes had a smile in them even when his mouth wasn't joining in.

Richard let his mouth catch up with his beaming eyes and nodded at Edna. "I have plenty of room for a big dog. And a yard!" he added.

Darlene gave Edna a look, wondering exactly what she was up to, but kept her mouth shut. Edna pointed at Gem's kennel.

The retriever had only been green-lighted for adoption for a few days, but for weeks she had been watching people walk by the kennels, stop and pet, and then take other dogs for walks out back. Sometimes the dogs left with the people. Sometimes they didn't.

Richard's grin grew even wider when his eyes locked on Gem. "Hey, girl!" he said softly. "Aren't you pretty!"

Gem walked closer to the fence. She sniffed the skinny man's hands, though she'd smelled him coming a mile away. He smelled *delicious*! Gem could not get her nose close enough.

"Wow!" Edna commented when Gem pushed her soft brown snout right up against the fencing. "You must have some sweet cologne."

Richard let out a great belly laugh. "I work at Hamburger Heaven," he said. "Or maybe they should call it Dog Heaven."

After a walk and a half hour of getting to know each other in one of the special rooms that was set up like a cozy living room in a house, Richard and Gem seemed like an ideal fit. It might have been the aroma of flame-broiled meat, or the fact that Richard quickly found the sweet spot behind Gem's ears, but Edna had never seen Gem so waggy!

"Do you want to come home with me?" Richard asked, looking into Gem's brown eyes. Gem wagged "yes," and Edna was so sure of the match she neglected to point out to Darlene that the letter from Richard's landlord said "small pets only." Gem was small, she told herself, for a golden retriever. A large golden could easily weigh seventy-five pounds. Gem was much closer to fifty.

🐾　🐾　🐾

Richard's one-bedroom house was as warm and welcoming and worn around the edges as he was. Gem felt comfortable in it immediately. He brought her two bowls and food and a bed and opened the back door to show her the fenced yard where she could relieve herself. When the sun went down, Richard plopped onto a sagging couch. Gem looked at him for a moment. She heard the mom's

voice in her head—"No dogs on the furniture"—
and pictured her angrily brushing dog fur off the
family's leather sofa. She started to circle, ready to
curl onto the floor, but Richard patted the cushion
beside him.

"Right here, Gemma!" he said. "I can't pet you if
you're so far away!"

Gem hopped up beside him and laid her head
in his lap. That night she slept curled beside him in
his bed. And for almost a week Gem didn't even
think about digging.

The nights at Richard's were Gem's favorite. Most
of the time Richard would bring her home a leftover hamburger. After they ate they liked to watch
TV, and Gem sprawled beside Richard on the
couch. Richard told her what was going on in his
favorite shows. Gem didn't really understand, but
she liked Richard's rumbly voice and the way he
laughed at the glowing screen. Every once in a
while the shows made him sad and Gem was there
to lick his face until he laughed again.

The days at Richard's were harder. Richard had to go to work, and he was gone for a long time. As the days went on, each seemed emptier and sadder than the one before . . . an endless stream of lonely. Before long, the lonely and the sad got the better of Gem. She wanted to claw it away. She wanted to bury it. Without even thinking she started to paw at the lumpy couch cushion. She scratched and clawed and dug, wanting to be somewhere different. Wanting to feel something different. The fabric split beneath her paws, revealing the fluffy insides. Gem tried to stop when she saw the stuffing, but couldn't. She kept digging paw over paw until the whole living room was covered with bits of foam and fuzz. The empty cushion sagged just like Gem's head when she looked around at what she had done.

Richard's jaw dropped when he got home. Gem, who usually greeted him at the door with wags and happy yips, hid under the table. She cowered, afraid to look at him, waiting to hear the words.

Bad dog. Richard didn't yell, though. Or use the words. He laughed. He laughed so hard and so long that Gem finally crawled out.

"Crazy pup!" Richard chuckled. He threw a blanket over the mess on the couch and patted the spot beside him. The next day, he cut a hole in the back door and put in a dog door—a flap that Gem could push open herself.

"Do your digging out here," Richard said, "okay?" The backyard was small. There weren't any rosebushes or flower beds, just hard-packed dirt and weeds. Gem gave a tentative scratch at the dried clay. Richard cheered her on. "That's it! Good dog!" Gem dug more . . . and more. Digging in the dried-up earth wasn't as fun as pawing through soft, freshly turned soil or damp sod, but hearing Richard tell her she was a good dog made the digging wonderful.

Gem loved Richard and their nights together, the leftover burgers and the walks after dark, sniffing the air for raccoons and possums. She liked sleeping in with Richard in the mornings. And she loved the belly rubs.

The days were still long and lonely, but when it was too much, she'd head outside and dig and dig and dig. It made her tired even when it didn't make her feel better.

One day—on one of Richard's days off—the two were flopped together on the couch when the doorbell rang. Gem barked—they didn't get many visitors—and Richard opened the door. A man who smelled like strong soap and a whiff of mildew was standing on the porch holding a metal box with a handle. Gem was surprised to see him. He looked surprised to see her, too.

"Thanks for coming!" Richard took the man's hand and smiled widely. The man did not smile back. He was staring at Gem. Richard kept talking. "The drip has been keeping us up at night, hasn't it, Gem?"

The man's eyes narrowed to slits. "Are you dog-sitting?" he asked.

Gem recognized a couple of his words and sat.

Richard kept smiling, but Gem could smell that it was a nervous smile and not a friendly one. "Oh, no. This is my dog, Gemma," he said, showing lots of teeth.

"Dog's not in the lease," the man growled. He pushed past them both and walked into the kitchen, where the tap was dripping. He set his metal box on the counter and stared at the back door. He walked over and pushed the dog door flap with his foot. "That's coming out of your deposit," he groused.

Richard let out a fake half laugh. "But it's an improvement! Now Gem can get out when I'm not home!"

The man opened the door. His face was so squished up, Gem wondered if he could see. She bounded out to her digging grounds to show him what a great place it was and looked back as if to say, "See?" But the man's expression did not change. He shut the door, and Gem heard his angry growl through the flap. It sounded like the mom's voice when she'd told her she was a bad dog. Gem curled up beside the prickly bush at the far end of the tiny yard and didn't go back inside until the angry man was gone and Richard was in the doorway calling her.

Gem walked slowly over to Richard. Something had changed. She could feel it. His ever-ready smile was gone, and not just from his lips. It was gone from his eyes, too.

That night and for the days that followed, Richard didn't take Gem on walks. He spent all his time on his phone and computer looking for a new home. His landlord had given him one week to get out or "get rid of the dog." The words echoed in his head and made it hard for him to look at Gem. He loved her. She'd made his life so much happier! And she hadn't done anything wrong.

Most of the places Richard found to rent were too expensive. The rest didn't allow dogs. On Friday, the last day he had to search, he brought

Gem three hamburgers and slept on the couch with the TV on. In the morning, he led Gem out to the car.

This time, Gem knew the big parking lot. She knew the sound of barking dogs. She knew the director's astringent smell and disappointed look. She knew she wasn't going to see Richard again. His cheeks were salty when he leaned down to say goodbye. She licked them and walked into a hard kennel like the one she'd been in when Richard found her. She lay down, not bothering to howl.

In the morning, Gem heard a familiar voice and let her tail thump. But only once. Edna.

The volunteer did a double take as Gem got slowly to her feet. "Gem?" Edna asked. The rosy golden retriever responded with two more slow wags. Edna wasn't sure what was more surprising: seeing the young dog back at the shelter, or seeing how much weight she had gained in such a short time. The once-slim pup had put on at least fifteen pounds. Her rounder body made her legs look short, and she moved without the spring she used to have in her step. But when Edna looked into those deep brown eyes, there was no denying this was the same sensitive dog she had befriended weeks before. "Oh, Gem," Edna said softly. "What are we going to do with you?"

04

Gem nosed the food in her bowl before burying her muzzle and eating the lot in a few bites. She licked her lips and looked at Edna, who had placed the bowl in her kennel only a minute before. "I know you want more," Edna said sympathetically. "Dieting is tough."

The dog's stomach complained loudly as Edna moved on to feed the next dog in the line of cages. Gem missed her hamburgers and her late-night walks and sleeping on a big comfy human bed. She also missed Richard. And the digging yard!

Though she'd been back at the shelter at least a week, Gem had been out with Edna only twice. She'd gotten excited when Edna opened the door to the outside dog area, but both times Edna seemed morc interested in keeping Gem walking than taking her to their digging spot. Gem didn't sleep as much with a grumbling belly and without the relief brought by an afternoon of digging. Her heart felt as heavy and as low as her tail. She didn't dare to hope that the people looking for dogs at the shelter might be looking for her.

Once, Edna brought a family around. They talked sweetly to Gem and were happy to read that she was good with kids. They asked Edna if they could take her out for a walk, but while Edna was getting a leash, the director came by. "You know she digs, right? Did Edna tell you about the digging?" The couple looked at each other, then back at Gem. They shook their heads slowly. Their faces dropped and so did Gem's tail. When Edna returned, they were looking at a Labradoodle two kennels down.

Edna pressed her lips together and looked at Gem's stats; there was more information on her clipboard now, including a glowing review from Richard about what a nice dog she was and her excellent companionship. But being returned after being adopted was a second strike against her. She'd been surrendered *twice*. And she was a digger, which fell under the category of "destructive behaviors." There weren't going to be many more chances for a dog like Gem.

If it had been up to Edna, she would have changed Gem's record to show just the first return. She felt guilty for having hidden the detail about Richard's landlord only wanting small pets. She knew "small pets" meant a cat or a gerbil or something. She thought she'd been doing the right thing.

"Someone will come," Edna whispered to Gem at the end of her shift. It was all she could do . . . all either of them could do. Just wait and hope.

☙ ☙ ☙

Juniper Sterling never really liked the term "lucky dog." It seemed to imply that all dogs were lucky. After spending her whole life on her family's ranch, the Sterling Center, where they trained dogs and people to do search and rescue, she'd seen *plenty* of unlucky dogs—dogs who'd been neglected or abandoned or deemed terrible pets. If these dogs made it to Sterling, their luck changed. Once they were Sterling dogs, even if they failed training, they wouldn't be put down. The team would find them a happy home. Somewhere. It was a promise they made. But a lot of dogs didn't make it to Sterling. A lot of dogs *were* put down. Juniper sniffed and eyed the row of cages and the hopeful dogs inside. They didn't look like "lucky dogs" to her.

Juniper preferred cats. Cats were the reason she'd come to the shelter in the first place. It had been a hard week, and she needed a powerful dose of kittens to make herself feel better. When she heard that Roxanne, the head trainer, was headed out for one of her regular shelter visits, Juniper surprised them both by asking if she could ride along. She already had the best cats in the world at home: a giant orange tabby named Twig and a gray furball named Bud. But there was nothing like getting some kitten fuzz up your nose.

So what was she doing in the canine kennels, when the kitty cages were just a doorway away? She wasn't sure exactly. She had followed Roxanne without thinking. And now here she was, standing outside a kennel reading a clipboard hanging on a young golden retriever's cage. "You're a digger, huh?" The highlighted behavior was hard to miss.

Lying on her bed, which was just a flattened pad in her kennel, Gem looked up. She heard the curiosity in the girl's voice. Her tail thumped, but she kept her head and her hopes down. So many people had peered at her through the fencing.

And as soon as they read whatever was written on the hanging board, they moved on.

"Gem?" Juniper read the name. "Here, Gem." She patted her leg, calling the dog.

Gem wondered if the girl would taste like Lexa— she smelled a little bit like her. Part of her wanted to walk over to the fence and lick her hand to find out. A bigger part was too afraid. She did not get up.

Juniper was used to this—her cats never came when she called, either. She half rolled her eyes and called again. Nothing. "Fine, then. I'll go see the kittens." Juniper turned, laughing, and Gem got up.

It was the laugh that got her—just like Lexa's. Gem stood and walked up to the gate.

Juniper turned back and grinned when she saw the dog wagging and walking to the fence. She looked into the pup's eyes—they were the color of dark caramel, warm with golden flecks. And there was something else about them—like if they were an actual pool of caramel that you could dive into, you wouldn't be able to touch the bottom. "So now you want to say hi?" She put her fingers through the cage.

Gem ducked her head and gave Juniper a lick. She tasted different from Lexa. More . . . animal. And a little salty and a little like gummy bears. Her giggle, though, was almost the same.

"Rough day?" Juniper asked. She couldn't stop staring at Gem's eyes. They weren't green, like Twig's, but they were nearly as expressive. She suddenly, desperately, wanted to get this dog out of her kennel. The urge was so strong it shocked her. After all, she was *not* a dog person.

"Who's this?" Roxanne came up behind Juniper and crouched down to look through the fencing at the reddish-gold retriever.

"This is Gem," Juniper introduced them. "Gem, this is Roxanne."

Roxanne gave the nine-year-old an amused and confused look. "I thought you didn't like dogs. I thought you were here for the cats."

Juniper shrugged. "Some dogs are special, I guess."

"Tell me about it." Roxanne flashed her a knowing smile.

Gem watched the people on the other side of the gate, one tall with a speckled face and the other smaller, like Lexa, and darker. They both had two braids, like tails by their ears, and they were both smiling—the human version of a wag. Gem's tail moved slowly at first and then faster the longer they stayed. She was curious about both of them. For one thing, they smelled like . . . dogs . . . and cats!

"Is it bad?" Juniper asked. "Being a digger?" She held the clipboard out to Roxanne, and pointed at the behavior listing on Gem's description card.

Roxanne pursed her lips. She looked at Gem thoughtfully. The dog was about the right age for search and rescue training. She was a bit overweight—though only a bit—and that was usually remedied easily with a diet. She had intelligent eyes. Plus, golden retrievers were a breed known for scenting skills and human bonding. "Digging isn't necessarily bad," Roxanne answered finally. "Sometimes it's a sign that a dog needs a job." She hesitated for a mere second, glanced at Juniper, and let her instincts take over. "Do you want to take Gem for a walk?"

05

"Yes!" Juniper replied, bouncing a little on her feet. "Yes, yes, yes!" She wanted to get that dog out of her kennel. She wanted to run her hands over Gem's rosy-gold fur. She wanted to get her away from all the unlucky dogs locked up around her.

Roxanne raised an eyebrow and chuckled at the youngest Sterling. She never knew what to expect from Juniper.

Edna, who had been pretending she wasn't watching the two visitors, approached with a leash and a smile. She'd liked them from the moment they came in. "You have excellent taste, ladies!" she said.

"Gem is a wonderful dog. Very loving, and very smart."

"Does she ever show aggression?" Roxanne asked. "With people, other dogs . . . or around food?"

Edna shook her head as she opened the kennel. "None of the above," she said. "She's a real sweetheart . . . a sensitive soul."

Edna focused on Gem. "Sit," she said. The young retriever lowered herself onto her haunches obediently and let Edna clip on the leash. The volunteer held it out to Roxanne, who gestured to the little girl with her chin. "I think Juniper can handle this one," she said. Juniper bit back a grin and took the leash.

Edna pointed to the door at the end of the row of kennels. "The dog run is through that door, and there are benches and places to sit and relax at the far end. Take your time out there. You can't rush getting to know one another!"

Juniper was already moving toward the door,

and Edna crossed her fingers. Gem was running out of options. She had a good feeling about these two visitors but knew it was just that—a feeling. It would take more than a few moments of warm, fuzzy emotions for Gem to find the right home. As Edna went back to caring for the other dogs, she said a silent prayer to the universe.

Roxanne watched the golden retriever carefully as she walked with Juniper. She'd been training dogs for nearly two decades and had a good sense of all kinds of breeds, personalities, and possible issues. Gem seemed like she needed reassurance, as many abused and rejected dogs did. She seemed to like Juniper, and perked up a bit with every step she took toward the door. Her tail, too, was on the rise, along with one of her golden ears. The other, it appeared, was permanently flopped.

Outside, Gem trotted along next to Juniper, who was talking a mile a minute. "I'm a cat person," Juniper confessed. "To be honest, I'm not even sure why I'm hanging out with you!"

Roxanne spotted a tug toy—a coiled rope with a loop at one end and a tennis ball at the other— lying in the dirt and bent to pick it up. One of the very first tests of SAR potential was seeing how curious and driven to play a dog was. It sounded a bit odd, but for most dogs, work and play were the same thing.

By the time Roxanne had straightened, Gem was right in front of her, eyeing the toy. She let out a little bark. "Can you unclip her, June?" the trainer asked. Juniper complied, and Roxanne waved the toy back and forth quickly. Gem followed it with her eyes for several seconds, getting more and more excited. Finally she lunged for the dingy ball.

"Off!" Roxanne said in a stern voice. A verbal correction needed to be clear—especially with a dog you didn't know well. It established that Roxanne was in charge, and gave the dog boundaries, assuming the dog had had enough training to know what boundaries were, or in this case what "off" meant. Roxanne didn't know whether Gem had completed any obedience training or whether she knew any commands—though she'd sat well for the shelter volunteer. Dogs who'd been moved around a lot and had unstable puppyhoods often didn't. But Roxanne's tone alone seemed to be enough to make Gem stop and sit. The dog shifted her gaze from the toy to Roxanne and back, trying to figure out what the woman wanted.

Roxanne smiled down at the eager-to-please pup and immediately tossed her the toy—a reward. So far, so good! Gem was interested in playing and seemed to know some basic commands—or was at least able to read body language. And even more important, she sat and looked into Roxanne's eyes when the trainer called her off. Gem *wanted* to understand. She wanted to please.

Juniper watched all of this, her expression uncharacteristically blank.

"You can go look at the cats now if you want," Roxanne told her, thinking the girl was finally getting bored. She was surprised the cat-crazy Sterling had deigned to linger this long with a hound. "Aren't you here to scout for the next feline phenom?"

Juniper, though, didn't budge. And she completely ignored the question. "So, that's good, right?" She pointed at Gem, who was still playing with the ball on a rope. "That the dog wants to play?"

Roxanne nodded. "Definitely." She glanced around the dog run, considering the next part of the assessment. "Do you want to help with the next bit? Try and hide the toy?" she asked.

Juniper flashed a rare smile and nodded emphatically. "Ohhhhh! So this will tell you if Gem sniffs as well as she digs!"

Roxanne nodded and skillfully distracted Gem from the toy so Juniper could retrieve it. The girl picked up the drooly ball and skipped to the end of the dog run, where there was a stand of evergreen shrubs. She buried the toy deep in the branches of the thickest one, ignoring the prickles.

She stepped back and peered into the bush from several angles. It wasn't visible at all.

As she returned to the spot where Roxanne and Gem were waiting, Juniper worried that maybe she'd hidden the toy too well. She wanted to challenge Gem. She also wanted to see her succeed! Her face scrunched up with worry.

"Okay, now let her smell your hands," Roxanne said. "So she can get the scent of the toy."

Juniper held out her hands. Gem stepped forward and pushed her dark nose into Juniper's open palms, going back and forth between them, huffing and snuffling. When she had gotten her fill, she stared up at Juniper and let out a bark. "Woof!"

Juniper shrugged in response, wiping her slightly damp hands on her jeans and then holding them out again, empty. "Where'd it go, Gem?" she asked. Gem didn't know what she was saying but liked her playful tone. "Go get it!" Juniper added.

Gem dashed away. She lifted her snout, sniffing,

and then put it to the ground. She followed her nose to the spot where Juniper had stashed the chewed-up tug rope. It took some determination—she had to shove herself into the poky hedge—but she finally got her teeth around the handle and yanked the toy out of its hiding place. She pranced back to the tall lady and the girl, looking pleased.

Roxanne nodded to herself. Gem's tail was waving proudly, like a flag in a breeze. The depressed dog in the kennel was nowhere to be seen.

Juniper was eyeing Roxanne. "So, are we taking her?" she asked.

Roxanne was thoughtful. "There's more to check out," she replied. She needed to make sure Gem didn't startle easily, for one. There wasn't anything in her history that would indicate she did, but it was always wise to check. She asked Juniper to take Gem to the bench about twenty yards away and distract her enough so that she didn't see Roxanne approach. When they were settled, Roxanne walked up and abruptly shrieked in mock alarm. Gem turned her head toward the trainer but remained calm and primarily focused on Juniper. A definite pass.

"Anything else?" Juniper wanted to know. "Can we take her now?"

Roxanne half wondered what would happen if she said no—Juniper's face wore a fighting-words look. For a nine-year-old, she was formidable. Luckily, Roxanne wasn't about to turn this dog down. She nodded, wearing a wide smile. "Yes, we can take her now."

06

Gem stood in the reception area of the shelter wagging and wagging and wagging. She couldn't believe that these people wanted to take her home! They smelled delicious . . . even better than Richard and his burger cologne! The smells of these two swirled together—gummy bears and dog and happy and cat—and made Gem's tail move back and forth extra fast! She licked Juniper's hand while Roxanne and the lady behind the desk took care of the paperwork.

Gem heard a door open and turned to see Edna hustling out of the kennel area, beaming and carrying the tug toy from the dog run, which Gem adored.

When she heard that Roxanne and Juniper were taking Gem home, and exactly what that home was, Edna's best hopes were realized. She'd watched the threesome outside through the small window in the door to the dog run, and was thrilled with what she saw. Roxanne very clearly knew dogs . . . and also loved them. Edna was filled with relief. The Sterling Center was a dream for a smart, sensitive pup like Gem. And now Edna understood that a job was what the golden retriever had needed all along! And on top of that, if Gem didn't become a search and rescue dog, the Sterling Center would let her stay with them until they found an appropriate home for her. It was really too good to be true!

When all the papers were filled out, Edna followed Roxanne and Juniper out to the parking lot. "Thank you so much," she said. "Gem is a special dog. She deserves a good life and a lucky break."

Roxanne reached out a hand to Edna. "No,

thank *you*," she said. "I think we might be the lucky ones."

Edna blinked back a tear as she crouched and buried her nose in the dog's silky fur. "I'm going to miss you, girl," she whispered. Then she laughed a little belly laugh. "Probably more than you'll miss me!"

Gem licked Edna's face again and again, leaning against her. Every lick was a thank-you. Then she and Edna played a final brief game of tug, which Gem won. Everyone watched her quick victory shake, and then Gem hopped into the back seat of Roxanne's truck with the toy in her mouth.

Edna stood up and saw right away that her black pants were covered in reddish-golden hair. A parting gift. She sighed and waved goodbye, happy to have a little bit of Gem still with her.

"What a great surprise," Roxanne said as they pulled out of the parking lot. The Sterling Center was always on the lookout for dog recruits and Roxanne visited shelters when she had extra time, though that wasn't often. Mostly their recruits were called in to *them*—someone had a pup who wasn't fitting in elsewhere or showed amazing promise, so they contacted the ranch and asked them to come evaluate. It was rare to bring a dog back from a casual look-see at a shelter.

"Hey . . . we didn't look at the cats!" Juniper exclaimed, suddenly realizing that she'd completely forgotten about her mission to snuggle a posse of kittens. How was that even possible? She never forgot about cats. Ever!

"That okay?" Roxanne asked.

Juniper nodded, surprised. It really was okay. Under normal circumstances, she would have been pouting about missing out on the felines or preparing to launch into a multipart argument about why they should turn back immediately—especially since she'd been in a terrible mood when they'd left the ranch and seeing kittens was her entire plan. But she wasn't. And she wasn't in a bad mood anymore, either. She was all smiles and excitement. She turned halfway around and reached an arm out to Gem, who was panting in the narrow back seat. There was something about this dog . . .

The car ride was longer than the one to Richard's—a lot longer. Gem rode in the center of the back seat, looking out the windshield between the tall lady and the girl. Neither of them talked much, but now and then Juniper would turn, put her hand on Gem's neck, and give a reassuring scratch.

When they finally stopped, Gem could tell right away that they were in a very big place. Roxanne let the pup out of the car, and Gem sniffed her way across the parking lot to a grassy area beside a building to relieve herself.

"Come on, Gem!" Juniper called. "We've got places to go and people and cats to meet!" She clipped a lead on the dog and opened the door, tugging Gem into a big reception area. It was kind of like the one at the shelter but also different. For one thing, it smelled like happy dogs, not fear. It also smelled like people.

Aromas of nail polish and coffee with sugar wafted off the girl behind the desk. "And who is *this*?" she wanted to know as she left her seat and came to greet Gem.

Juniper planted her hands on her hips. "This is Gem!" she announced. "And don't get too attached, Shelby. *I* found her!" She crouched down next to Gem and whispered, "That's Shelby, my oldest sister. She thinks she knows everything."

Another, older person with a halo of long, dark hair came out of a small room next to the reception and peered curiously at Gem.

"Mom! Look!" Juniper crowed. Then she cleared her throat, as if remembering her manners. "Gem, this is my mother, Georgia. She is in charge of pretty much everything around here." She grimaced. "Especially me."

Georgia smiled. "You got that right," she said, winking at her youngest. "Nice to meet you, Gem." Georgia bowed her head a little in greeting. Gem was about to step closer and rub a few hairs onto the woman's long skirt when another woman came in. She had short white hair and pale skin and seemed surprised to see the crowd in the reception room.

"Well, hello!" she chirped.

Juniper turned slightly. "Grandma! You're just in time! I'm doing introductions! Gem, this nice lady is my grandmother Frances." She gestured back toward her mother, who was still enjoying the scene. "Frances is my dad's mom. She started this whole entire place, but now Mom runs it and Grandma is retired. Mostly."

The women all laughed at that, but Gem wasn't really listening. She was lifting her nose past Frances to the big, slow-moving chocolate Lab who had followed her in and was sniffing her way over. "Be nice to Gem, Cocoa," Juniper told the big brown dog, though Cocoa was the calmest dog on the ranch . . . and the oldest. Cocoa sized up Gem, giving her a good sniff. Her eyes were starting to get a little milky, but her nose still worked great.

Gem sniffed back, and both tails wagged in unison.

"Where are Bud and Twig?" Juniper wanted to know. "I *have* to introduce them to Gem!"

Shelby shrugged. "Probably giving each other makeovers in your room. You know, in preparation for their upcoming movie careers." The corners of her lips twitched upward into a smirk, making Juniper scowl.

"Not funny, Shelby," Juniper protested while the others tried to hide their giggles. "Come on, Gem," she said, tugging lightly on the leash. "I have better things to do than stand here and be ridiculed by Shel-beeeeee." Juniper flounced toward the door, and Gem happily trotted beside her, toenails clicking on the tile floor.

Roxanne shot a quick glance over her shoulder at the trio of ladies and went after Juniper and Gem despite the fact that she hadn't exactly been invited.

Outside, the girl-and-dog duo didn't get far

before they ran into two men working on some kind of giant digging machine. "This is Gem," Juniper announced proudly. "I picked her." The two men shared a look of amused surprise. Roxanne raised her brows in their direction but didn't correct the youngest Sterling.

"Gem, this is Pedro." She pointed to the shorter man with a close-trimmed beard, who crouched down in front of Gem to say hello. "He's in charge of the people who come to work with the dogs." The bearded man held his hand out gently, and Gem gave it several licks. He tasted like Takis!

"And this is my dad, Martin." Juniper pointed to the other, taller man. He had short whitish hair, and not much of it. "He is in charge of all the machines and buildings on the ranch." She waved a hand all around the big place, gesturing to the buildings. Then her eyes settled on the excavator and she let out a hoot of laughter. "Hey, Dad, they say Gem is a digger! Just like your machine!"

Martin half smiled and shook his head. "We just

might need her services, then, if we can't get this thing fixed. It's been making me crazy for the past week. I can't figure out what the problem is!"

"Oh, well, I'm sure Gem could handle any digging for you," Juniper said, petting the dog proudly. "According to the notes on the clipboard at the shelter, she's obsessive! But that little obsession is part of what will make her a great SAR dog."

Martin gazed at his daughter—the one he had helped search and search for her missing cat, the one who made him watch hours of cat-training YouTube videos, the one who claimed dogs were overrated and undersmart. "Who are you and what did you do with my cat-loving June Bug?" he asked with mock seriousness.

Juniper rolled her eyes. "Daaaad. I am right here!" she said. "And I am still one hundred percent dedicated to my kitties. Gem is just . . . special."

Martin nodded gravely. "Obviously."

Juniper waited expectantly until Pedro and Roxanne nodded their agreement as well.

"And now for the best part, Gemmy," Juniper said, moving on. "The canine pavilion!" She led the new recruit to a big door in a big building. Inside was the biggest, best place that Gem had ever seen that didn't have dirt for digging.

Two kids were working near a row of kennels. They both glanced up when the door opened, and Gem smelled their surprise. She'd been smelling surprise since she got here!

The two kids stopped what they were doing and hurried over to meet the dog. Juniper let out a puff of air, as if she were tired of introductions. "Who is *this* gorgeous pup, Roxanne?" Morgan asked, ignoring her sister and bending down to look into Gem's eyes.

"She's a looker for sure . . ." Forrest nodded approvingly. "And sweet," he added when Gem licked him for the compliment.

"This is Gem. *I* found her at the shelter . . . didn't I, Roxanne?"

"You sure did," Roxanne agreed, giving Forrest

and Morgan a wink. "Gem has a good nose, and it would seem Juniper has a good nose for finding new recruits, too."

"Gem, this is Forrest and this is Morgan." She motioned at the boy and girl in turn, then shook her head, making her braids swish. "They're both older than me. *Everyone* is older than me."

Gem took her time sniffing the new kids. They smelled like books, and dogs, and peanut butter, and soccer fields—all things Gem liked. So far, Gem liked everything about this place. This building was sort of like the shelter, with kennels and bins of food and leashes, but also *not* like the shelter, because the people and the dogs were happy. There was not a whiff of fear or sorrow. None of the dogs were whining, or barking and barking and barking, or lying limply on their beds like unstuffed squeaky toys. This place smelled like . . . joy.

"Where's her food?" Juniper asked. "I want to feed Gem her first meal on the ranch."

Morgan narrowed her eyes a little suspiciously, as this was not typical Juniper behavior. She rarely stepped foot inside the canine pavilion, unlike her and Forrest, who worked there every day before and after school and on weekends. Morgan and her next oldest sibling could not get enough of dogs! Still, Morgan didn't tease. She generally admired her little sister's utter dedication to whatever it was she decided to dedicate herself. Juniper did not mess around! Morgan glanced up and got an "okay" nod from Roxanne.

"Come on, I'll show you," she said, waving her toward the area of the pavilion that housed the dog food.

The sisters fed Gem together, and while the dog ate, Morgan set up a kennel. After she finished eating, Juniper escorted Gem inside and led her to her thick, comfy bed, giving her soft fur a final pet for the day. "I think you're going to like it here," she whispered in Gem's ear. Gem sighed and rested her head on her paws. She thought so, too.

07

Juniper opened her eyes before the sun came through her window, her brain full of Gem. She couldn't remember the details, but she was pretty sure she'd just been dreaming about the golden dog. Something about a picnic with gourmet cat and dog treats? She shook her head to rid herself of the fuzzy images and gently scooched Bud and Twig off her pillow.

"Good morning, gentlemen!" she said as they settled back down. She hopped out of bed, hurriedly pulling on her favorite jeans and a sweatshirt, and felt a tiny tug of guilt for wanting to see Gem so badly when the loves of her life were right here. She quickly brushed the feeling aside.

"Who wants breakfast?" she asked before heading downstairs.

The cats lazily got to their feet and stretched—it was early, but they didn't like to miss food—and jumped down onto the shaggy carpet Juniper kept next to her bed. Bud paused to lick a fuzzy white paw.

"Meow," Twig complained, protesting the early wake-up on a Sunday.

"I know," Juniper agreed, bending to scoop him into her arms for a cuddle. "But I have to go somewhere." She tromped down the stairs and into the kitchen with Twig in her arms and Bud on her heels. She filled their bowls with kitty kibble, then added a scoop of wet food on top . . . giving them both a little extra. The moment their bowls were on the ground, she dashed out the door to the canine pavilion. Her body felt kind of tingly, like it did on her birthday before she blew out the candles. She couldn't wait to see Gem!

Inside, Morgan and Forrest were already hard at work, doing the daily morning chores of feeding and watering and walking the dogs. They didn't expect anyone to come through the door this early on a Sunday, and when they saw it was Juniper, they couldn't hide their surprise.

"What are you doing here?" Forrest asked. Morgan just blinked and tossed her hair twists out of her eyes.

Juniper ignored them both and beelined to Gem's kennel. When Gem saw her, she got to her feet and came to the kennel door, wagging. She licked Juniper's kitty-kibble-flavored hand through the chain link.

"Good morning, Gemmy!" Juniper crooned. She put her face right up to the fencing to get an up-close lick. "Oh, I missed you, too!"

Morgan and Forrest watched in shock. Finally, Juniper turned in their direction. "I'm here to take care of my dog," she announced.

Morgan and Forrest exchanged a long look

before Morgan said what they were both thinking: "You know none of the dogs are *ours*, right?" she asked gently. "They're here to train so they can go out into the world and help people . . ."

Juniper huffed a little and rolled her eyes. "Okay, fine. But I'm still here to take care of Gem." She started toward the cupboard that held the bins of food.

"You're not old enough to handle dog care," Forrest blurted. It was just like Juniper to jump in and take over. He and Morgan had asked repeatedly and waited and *earned* the chance to work in the canine pavilion, and she just marched in like she owned the place . . . or at least one of the dogs . . . who weren't even ownable! Juniper could really get under his skin.

Seeing the hackles rising on both her siblings, Morgan stepped in. She never liked a fight and knew exactly how stubborn both of them could be . . . especially when dealing with each other. She shot Forrest a heavy sideways glance and hoped he got her unspoken message to keep quiet. She was the one to handle this.

Forrest shot her a look back that said something a lot ruder.

"Let me show you how the food works, okay?" Morgan said, and then kept talking so her headstrong sister wouldn't have a chance to answer. "Every dog has his or her own regimen. Most of them share the same food, but they get different amounts, and some are on supplements or have dietary restrictions . . ." She pointed to a whiteboard that listed each dog's name beside the type of food they ate, and his or her portion size. Next to that was another whiteboard with additional notes or special instructions from Roxanne or Dr. Jessica, the ranch's on-call vet, about supplements and allergies. Every dog had his or her own section.

"I only care about Gem," Juniper announced when Morgan was finished.

"Gem is just one of the dogs," Forrest said a little

hotly. Who did she think she was, flouncing in here and acting like she was in charge? Or thinking that not every dog deserved special care?

Morgan sighed and rolled her eyes at Forrest behind Juniper's back.

Juniper ignored her brother but followed her sister's instructions and prepared Gem's morning meal.

The new dog was licking the bowl clean when Roxanne arrived. The lead trainer did a double take when she spotted Juniper, then smiled to herself. The spell that Gem cast on the cat lover was still working.

"Roxanne!" Juniper said, running up to her. "Gem and I are ready to get to work!" Roxanne drew in a breath. Juniper's insistence on being involved posed a very clear dilemma. At nine, Juniper was too young to work as a training assistant. The Sterlings weren't a rule-crazy family, but the ranch did have a few well-established guidelines when it came to working with the animals. Georgia was a firm believer in clear boundaries for kids *and* for dogs, and claimed that without them it would be chaos.

And that wasn't all. Roxanne also suspected that Juniper was too . . . she tapped her chin and tried to think of the right word—Exuberant? Impatient? Dramatic?—to work with the dogs. Perhaps it was all of the above.

"Hell-oooo." Juniper waved a hand in front of the lost-in-thought trainer. "You in there?"

Roxanne refocused on Juniper's expectant face. Juniper, the only Sterling child who had never expressed the slightest interest in dogs. Juniper, now earnestly and enthusiastically taking an interest . . . and Forrest staring daggers, waiting to see what Roxanne said next.

"I'm thinking," Roxanne answered honestly.

Juniper dropped her hands to her sides in disappointed impatience but didn't say anything else while Roxanne continued to mull it over.

It was Sunday, which was generally a rest day on the ranch. The dogs always needed care, but they didn't do extra work or train on Sundays. Usually. In fact, most Sundays, Roxanne didn't even make it to the pavilion. Today, though, she had wanted to spend a moment with Gem and see what the new dog was all about . . . what kind of potential she had . . . what she was like away from the shelter. She glanced at Juniper, who was clearly struggling to keep her mouth closed as she rocked back and forth on the balls of her feet.

Roxanne knew she'd have to talk to the adult Sterling team—Pedro and Georgia and Martin—about how to involve Juniper. But for now she decided to go with her gut, which was telling her to allow Juniper to come with her and Gem out to the training grounds at least this once. It would give her a chance to see how the kid did out there. They could try some obedience work . . . nothing big. For all she knew, Juniper would get bored or decide she needed to make some movie-industry calls on behalf of her cats before lunchtime arrived, in which case that would be that.

"Okay, you can come out with me and Gem to the training grounds," Roxanne agreed.

Juniper lunged forward and threw her arms around Roxanne. "Oh, thank you, thank you, THANK you!"

Morgan shook her head lightly in surprise. Of all the people on the ranch, Roxanne was the least likely to be manipulated by Juniper. Forrest looked like he'd swallowed a bee, but held his tongue.

Roxanne pulled a lead off a hook on the wall, and the threesome departed, leaving Morgan and Forrest to gape and grumble.

When they arrived at the training grounds, Roxanne asked Gem to sit before turning to Juniper. "Okay, I'm going to do some basic obedience stuff, and I'd like you to stand over by the grass and watch. Sound okay?"

Juniper nodded. She was disappointed and walked slowly (for Juniper) to the edge of the official training area. Roxanne already had Gem in a sit, which she had demonstrated at the shelter, so they quickly moved on to the next command: stay.

"Stay," Roxanne said in her command voice— clear and firm. Then she started to walk.

Gem wagged and wagged as Roxanne moved farther away. Her hindquarters wiggled a little on the ground, and her eyes stayed fixed on Roxanne. Juniper stifled a giggle as she watched. Despite her little wriggles, Gem stayed put until she was called, and even managed, by the sixth try, to actually hold still.

"Good stay," Roxanne called. "Come!" Gem rose to her feet and scampered over to the trainer, receiving her treat and, eventually, a good tug game with the dingy but beloved toy Edna had given them before they left the shelter. Roxanne repeated the three skills more than she usually did. It was a trick she used sometimes to determine how easily a dog got bored. Today, though, she was assessing Juniper.

Juniper was focused. She watched the session in silence, making mental notes the whole time. She'd seen dog training before, of course . . . Her family owned a dog-training ranch! She couldn't miss it if she'd wanted to. She'd even tried to glean training tips from Roxanne in the hopes of using them on her beloved kitties. But somehow this felt different. It felt more important. More exciting. And a lot more fun.

Gem was *definitely* having a good time. Training was like a big game. It didn't take her long to understand what the tall, freckled lady wanted her to do—or to learn that when she did the right thing, she got to eat a treat and play tug! She was so busy having fun she almost didn't notice that the ranch was covered in dirt she could dig.

Almost.

08

"I'm starved," Juniper said as she and Morgan headed toward their house. The colder fall weather made her extra hungry. "I hope dinner is something good!" She pushed open the back door and the smell of baking lasagna—her mother's specialty—hit her nose. If she were a dog she would have drooled. She took off her sneakers and was about to shout out that they were home when something made her clamp her mouth closed instead. There was a conversation going on in the dining room . . . one that sounded grown-up and serious.

Putting a finger to her lips and opening her eyes wide to make sure Morgan got the message, Juniper stepped into the kitchen in her stocking feet and made her way on tiptoes to the far wall. Morgan followed silently, and they stood together near the door to the dining room, eavesdropping.

"She did remarkably well, really. Much better than I expected," Roxanne said. The adults around the table all chuckled, and the spying girls listened carefully to try and figure out who was in the next room. Roxanne . . . their parents . . . maybe Pedro . . .

"It makes sense on many levels." Their dad's voice was unmistakable. "She has a determined spirit. It wouldn't be like her to do things halfway."

"I am honestly surprised by her focus. It's not like she's experienced a lot of training," Roxanne responded.

Juniper heard a tapping noise—drumming her finger was something her mom did when she was thinking. Then she heard her mom's voice. "It is an unexpected twist," she said. "And there will have to be some adjustments—we hadn't planned on starting any new training right now. But my gut says we should go with it."

"Okay, so are we saying we will get started training, with Morgan helping out?" Martin asked.

On the other side of the wall, Juniper's face fell. Her mouth dropped open in dismay. Hadn't she made clear to Roxanne that *she* wanted to help train Gem?

"I think so," Roxanne said. "Morgan is the right choice to offer guidance and assistance. She's very knowledgeable and patient. Maybe she can translate some of that to the, uh, new recruit."

Juniper couldn't believe what she was hearing. It was so unfair! Her sister always got to participate in training! It took just a few seconds for her sadness to turn to anger. Her gaping mouth slammed shut, and she set her jaw. Gem was *her* dog! *She'd* found her! *She'd* helped bring her to the ranch. Before she knew what was happening, she barged into the dining room, hands on her hips and ready for battle.

"It's always Morgan!" she shouted. "Morgan the dog queen! Gem is *my* dog! I found her, and I want to help train her!"

Georgia sat back in her chair, directing a look of dismay at her youngest. "Would you like to take a seat and join the conversation, Juniper?" she asked pointedly. "After a couple of deep breaths, perhaps?" She crossed her arms to clarify that she was not merely making a suggestion. This was an order.

Juniper took a breath in, let it out in a noisy huff, and slid into a seat at the table. She hated deep breaths and also hated that they actually worked. Parents knew too much . . . especially *hers*.

Martin smiled across the table at his firecracker daughter, then turned toward the door she'd just come through. "Anyone else in the kitchen?" he called.

Morgan's flowered sock appeared around the corner, followed slowly by the rest of her. She glanced at the adults apologetically and crept in to take her own seat at the table.

Georgia hid her knowing smile and cleared her throat lightly. "Perfect, you're both here. I'm not sure how long you ladies were"—she cleared her throat again—"*listening*, but we've decided that you, Juniper, have demonstrated both the necessary interest and the determination needed to work with Gem."

Juniper's head shot up, and she did an excited butt wiggle in her chair. "Really?" she asked, swallowing the mad that had gotten stuck in her throat.

Roxanne nodded. "We'd like you to be Gem's training assistant."

Juniper wriggled some more. "Really? Really?! But you said . . ."

"Yes, really." Roxanne turned to Morgan. "But since you are still very young we were thinking that Morgan could work alongside you. If she's willing?" Roxanne looked at the older girl. "As a sort of training coach?"

Morgan hesitated. She was relieved to be included and also a little nervous. She was an avid dog person and read a ton about dogs and training, but had always been the student . . . never the teacher. She glanced over at Juniper, who was squirming like the warty toads Forrest used to catch. Juniper—who usually dismissed dogs to the same degree that Morgan adored them—was the last person she expected to have as a dog-training student! Still, it was an interesting opportunity, and any time with the dogs was time well spent.

"Of course," she finally replied, smiling and trying not to show her nervousness. The table grew quiet with anticipation. It had been decided, but everyone was thinking the same thing. No matter how it all turned out, it was going to be an adventure for all of them!

🐾 🐾 🐾

Juniper hopped out of bed on Friday morning more quickly than she had since Gem arrived. It was a school day, and she had a *lot* to do before she caught the bus!

"Reow!" Twig complained. He still didn't appreciate being shoved off the bed at five thirty in the morning . . . not one bit. Luckily, Bud was a little more accepting, and neither was upset enough to scratch about it. Bud landed on the floor with a soft thump and proceeded with his brief grooming routine while Juniper got dressed. Juniper felt the usual twinge of kitty-abandoning guilt as she hurried down the stairs, but thinking about her time with Gem quickly eclipsed any negative feelings.

"Morning!" she chirped to her mom, who was already at the stove stirring a pot of oatmeal. She fed the kitties, splitting an entire can of cat food between them on top of their kibble. Once the bowls had been placed on the floor, she started for the door. Georgia held her back with four words . . . one of them in her second language, German.

"Breakfast, Schatz. *Before* Gem."

Juniper was tempted to argue but knew better. Her mama didn't sway easily, and when she spoke German she was usually serious, even when she was calling her "Sweetheart." Juniper climbed onto a stool at the counter and added brown sugar, milk, and raisins to her oatmeal. The warm cereal was gone in three minutes, and so was Juniper. "Bye!" she shouted over her shoulder. She was in such a hurry she didn't even notice that Bud was following her.

Gem smelled Juniper before the door to the canine pavilion even opened, and happily thumped her tail on her bed. Juniper reminded the pup of Lexa, her first girl, the one who used to let her sneak onto the big bed at night . . . even though it was against the rules. But this new girl was different. Juniper didn't sneak Gem into bed, so that was one difference. Another was their smell. Lexa had smelled like hand lotion and strawberry lip gloss. Gem preferred Juniper's smell: gummy bears and *cat*. She also liked that Juniper came to see her every day, even early in the mornings when she had school. She snuggled with Gem on *Gem's* bed. *And* Juniper read her stories.

Gem sniffed the air as her tail continued thumping. The scent of cat was stronger than ever today! It didn't take long to figure out why . . . a fluffy gray kitty was trotting right behind Juniper, trying to keep up.

"Good morning, my love!" Juniper singsonged as she stopped in front of her kennel. Gem looked at Juniper and then down at the cat by her feet. Following the dog's gaze, Juniper saw—and then felt—Bud weaving around her ankles. Her hand went to her mouth with embarrassment. She bent to scoop the cat into her arms. "I guess you were bound to find out about my dog love sometime, Buddy-boy!"

Juniper carried the cat into the kennel and set him down. "Bud, meet Gem. Gem, this is Bud." Gem thumped and thumped as she sniffed Bud's fuzzy gray ear. Bud pretended to be indifferent, then raised his tail and turned his backside toward the dog's curious nose.

"Are you ready for this morning's story?" Juniper settled herself onto Gem's bed, and though Bud didn't join them, he did sit against the kennel wall and listen to *Harry the Dirty Dog*—Juniper always chose the stories from a stack of old favorite picture books. She hadn't heard this one in years! They were on the last page when the door swung open and Morgan and Forrest came in for chores.

Gem rose and stretched, ready for breakfast and fresh water. Bud skittered out of the kennel while Juniper went to fill Gem's bowl with kibble. She was topping it off with a third scoop when Forrest looked her way.

"Hey, that's too much!" He pointed at the whiteboard. "Gem is supposed to get two scoops. The bowl should only be half-full. If you're going to do *our* job, you'd better do it right!"

Morgan saw Juniper's shoulders tense in frustration. "I know it's tempting to give extra food, but we need to keep the dogs in top working condition," she added gently, shooting Forrest a "be nice" look. "It's not really a treat, because it makes it harder for them to train and be their best."

"These dogs are fit!" Forrest chided. "Not like your overstuffed cats."

Juniper scowled as she scooped some of the kibble back out of the bowl. "Fine, but my cats are plenty fit!" She stuck her tongue out at Forrest and gave the remeasured bowl of food to Gem, comforting herself with how happy the pup seemed as she crunched her kibble. Forrest could say whatever he wanted. *He* wasn't the one who got to help train Gem. *She* was.

09

Pedro hit send on the email he'd finished, closed his laptop, and looked out the window of his trailer. Even in November, when the grassy hills were brown and the live oaks and evergreens were wearing their muted fall colors, the ranch was a beautiful place. From his perch on the hill at the back of the multi-acre property Pedro could see almost all of it—the cluster of buildings, the wide training grounds, the reconstructed "disaster areas"—and it was one of his favorite sights. He took a last swig of sweetened coffee and grabbed his work jacket from the hook by the door. He was a little late to meet Roxanne. They were getting together so he could observe the new dog, Gem, a pup who had the whole ranch talking. If she was as smart as everyone said, it wouldn't be long before he'd need to get her the perfect handler and SAR partner.

Though Pedro's role on the ranch was to train the humans who worked with the dogs, one of the biggest parts of the job, in his mind, was matchmaking. Pedro liked to create ideal dog-and-human duos. Although he ultimately had no say about whether a dog hit it off with the people he found or trained, he liked to think he had a sixth sense about these things and hated leaving either partner hanging. But every dog and every person had specific skills and quirks that made putting them together like locking in the right pieces of a puzzle.

This morning he'd been corresponding with a woman who wasn't going to require much in the way of training. Laurel Leon had been a SAR dog handler before, and according to her email, she was ready to be one again. She was a ranger and emergency medical technician who worked for the state parks near Carpinteria, California, on the coast. She was also a former lifeguard, and from the sound of it, she moved from land to water as easily as a Labrador retriever!

In fact, a Labrador was the dog Pedro was already imagining for her. After losing her last SAR dog, a Newfoundland named Bluto, she would need a different breed . . . but one with a huge heart and possibly webbed feet!

After reading the answer to one of his standard handler interview questions—*Tell me about a typical day in your life*—Pedro was certain that Laurel needed a water dog, which would probably make finding the right pup a little trickier than usual.

Water training was not something the Sterling ranch often did, for two reasons: (1) Although their training areas included a crashed airplane, an overturned bus, and a fake earthquake site, they did not have a lake or even a pond on the ranch.

And (2) it wasn't easy to find dogs who were as comfortable in water as they were on land.

Still, he was determined to find Laurel the right partner no matter how long it took, which was what he'd told her in his morning's email.

Pedro quickened his step and let his thoughts unroll. Normally he cautioned handlers not to rush back in with a new dog too quickly after their partner had passed or retired. Laurel, though, seemed to have taken this advice already. She'd written that it had been two years since she'd lost Bluto, who had died suddenly of an undetected heart problem. Bluto's sudden death had caught her off guard and, she confessed, thrown her into a bit of a tailspin.

After two years I finally feel like myself again, mostly, she'd typed in her email. *There is still a big piece of me that feels like it's missing. I am not trying to* replace *Bluto . . . there was only one of him. But it's time for me to find a new dog partner. I hope you can help.*

He appreciated that Laurel would not be

entering into a new canine partnership lightly. From her messages and a single phone conversation, he could tell she was smart, capable, and kind. Pedro hoped he could help.

🐾　🐾　🐾

Standing on the big training ground, it was difficult to determine who was most excited. Morgan, who was always thrilled to be out and working with dogs, was sporting a huge grin. Juniper was practically vibrating. And Gem was wagging so hard her whole back end was swaying from sidc to side. Roxanne beamed at all of them, shook her head, and wondered what she had gotten herself into. Had it really been her idea to work with two kids and a dog all at once? Of course, Morgan was as good as any of the paid assistants who worked on the ranch. Roxanne wondered if the magic touch Morgan had with dogs would also work on her little sister.

"I'm so glad we're on break!" Juniper said, hopping from one foot to the other. Her excited movements were getting Gem excited, too. She let out a woof.

"It's great timing," Roxanne agreed. The girls had a week off for Thanksgiving—time enough to give both Juniper and Gem a crash course. Today they would be starting with some repetitive obedience stuff and a little tracking. Roxanne wanted to see just how strong a scenter Gem was, and also wanted to demonstrate for Pedro what she suspected Gem's best talents to be.

She waved to Pedro before he stepped inside the observation trailer that was situated on the edge of the training grounds. The portable structure had a large window along one side that would allow Pedro to watch everything without being a distraction. Roxanne knew Pedro would be paying attention to how Gem interacted with people. Fortunately, despite being surrendered to a shelter twice, trust did not seem to be an issue for Gem. Still, being able to trust didn't always translate into strong bonds and connections.

"Let's start with basic obedience commands,"

Roxanne said. Morgan gave a nod and started to instruct Juniper on the proper hand signals to accompany her requests of Gem.

"I knooooow," the younger girl said, rolling her eyes.

"Okay, show me." Morgan was all business.

Juniper deftly ran through a series of commands with Gem: "sit," "stay," "come," and "down."

Growing up on a dog-training ranch had worn off on Juniper more than either Roxanne or Morgan would have thought. The youngest Sterling knew quite a lot! There was no denying that the girl and the dog were both impressive.

"Don't give her too much praise—it'll go to her head," Morgan whispered while Juniper kept Gem in a sit/stay.

Roxanne squinted, perplexed. It really wasn't possible to *over*praise a dog. Then she chuckled, realizing that Morgan was talking about her little sister! The trainer swallowed her laughter and gave a quick nod.

"You're doing great," she said loudly to the whole team. "Let's try something new. Can I borrow your scarf, Juniper?" The new assistant untied the bandanna she'd been wearing over her braids and held it out to Roxanne.

"Do you think she's ready to find?" Morgan asked, looking surprised.

"Only one way to *find* out!" Roxanne answered with a smirk. Morgan grinned and pulled Juniper aside to explain what they were going to do next while Roxanne led Gem in the other direction.

Gem looked up at Roxanne as she trotted alongside her. She liked playing with this tall lady and the girls. She liked their games. Even when they played the same thing over and over! She was ready for whatever was coming next. Roxanne walked with Gem for a long time without asking her to do anything, but Gem could tell something was coming. She could tell by the way Roxanne kept glancing around, the slight smile on her face and the way she stood extra straight. *And* she could tell by her excited smell. Finally, Roxanne asked Gem to heel, and then sit. She squatted down and held the square of fabric in her hand near Gem's nose. Gem sniffed it: Juniper! It smelled just like her favorite girl.

"Good!" Roxanne praised Gem when she buried her nose in the cloth. The tall lady straightened. Gem sat still and stared up at her expectantly. She wanted to wriggle but sat still and waited.

"Now. Find!" Roxanne said firmly.

Gem recognized Roxanne's command voice, but the command was not one Gem had heard before.

Roxanne held out the fabric and a fresh burst of "Juniper" wafted into Gem's nose. "Find," Roxanne repeated.

Inside Gem's head, something clicked. Roxanne was asking her to go after the smell. She wanted her to "find" Juniper!

The clever dog was off like a shot. She zigzagged across the field. She held her snout up high, pulling smells from the air, and pushed it back to the ground, where she could smell Juniper's tracks. She ran back and forth, picking up the path and losing it and finding it once more. The smells grew stronger and stronger until—

"Gem! You did it! You found me, Gem!" Juniper popped out from behind a fallen tree in the woods on the edge of the ranch. The girl and the dog jumped all over each other in celebration.

"That was super fast, wasn't it?" Morgan asked Roxanne in a side whisper as they approached. Roxanne nodded. She hadn't been timing, but she could safely say that was one of the most successful and speediest first finds she'd seen in a long time. Maybe ever.

Pedro jogged up a moment later. He was wearing a big grin that grew bigger when he saw Gem playing tug with her "victim," Juniper. "Looks like your instincts were right on this one, Rox," he said, impressed. "Her nose is exceptional!"

"Juniper's or Gem's?" Morgan cracked.

"Both!" Roxanne replied, not joking.

"I think you mean *my* instincts, Pedro!" Juniper yelled, having heard. "*I* picked her!"

Pedro called the dog to him and knelt down to pet her. Gem greeted him easily though they hadn't met before, and within seconds was leaning in for more rubbing and admiration. "I can't wait to see what else this dog can do," Pedro told the training team.

"Gem can do *anything*!" Juniper bragged.

Pedro stroked his beard thoughtfully for a second. Something was coming together in his head . . . clicking into place. "You might be right about that, Juniper Sterling!"

10

"Nothing like an impromptu field trip!" Roxanne called when Pedro pulled up the next morning in a white van towing a trailer.

Pedro leaned out the driver's window and patted the door emblazoned with the Sterling Center logo. "Let's get this show on the road!" He was smiling so widely he looked like a kid in a candy store.

When Pedro had suggested they take a water trip with dogs the day before, Roxanne thought he was joking. It was November! They were short-staffed because their assistant trainer Eloise was away, spending the holiday with her family, and water trips were a little bit complicated. But Roxanne had been working with Pedro long enough to know that everything he did, he did with intention. He hadn't made the suggestion lightly, and there were extra Sterlings around since the kids were on break. So she'd agreed.

Martin got out of the passenger side of the van and checked the tow hitch one last time. He'd been surprised, too, when Pedro had requested that the van and the Zodiac both be prepped for an outing. They didn't use the inflatable boat too often, and Martin hadn't been anticipating any water training until spring, so it was flat, dry, and packed up tight in one of the ranch's storage buildings.

The Sterling crew liked to expose the dogs to water at least once during the course of their time on the ranch, and sometimes they discovered that a dog had a real talent for water searches. Dogs with this kind of skill could actually smell things hundreds of feet below the surface! Martin, who was always game for a little time away from his maintenance tasks, hadn't hesitated when he got the request for a water field trip. He was more than happy to get the gear ready and make sure the training team had what they needed. If it were possible, he would have dug them a lake on the ranch or created a slope covered in fake snow for avalanche searching! He took real pride in making sure that the ranch provided the best, most realistic training facilities available.

Roxanne opened the sliding side door on the van and called back toward the pavilion. "Who's ready?"

The door burst open, and Juniper, Morgan, and Forrest emerged with three dogs wearing vests, leashes, and massive doggy grins.

The pups—Captain, Sally, and Gem—had no idea where they were headed, but they could pick up on the excitement of the humans and eagerly jumped into the waiting vehicle, tongues lolling.

"This is good for them," Morgan said to Juniper when everyone was buckled in, including the dogs, who had tether points on the side of the van.

"SAR dogs have to be comfortable in all modes of transportation," Roxanne added.

"Planes, trains, and automobiles," Forrest said, keeping one hand on Sally, a mixed spaniel with brown spots on white fur, floppy ears, and deep brown eyes. "And don't forget helicopters."

"Or boats," Juniper said, getting the last word and letting them all know that she didn't need schooling. Forrest scowled.

While he drove, Pedro listened to Roxanne go over exactly what the rest of the day would entail. The dogs would be introduced to the lake and invited to explore, and then they would put them on the Zodiac. The small craft was tippy, and some dogs would refuse. Once people and dogs were loaded, they would take them out to deep water and have the dogs jump overboard, swim, and come back aboard. In shallower water, the team would test to see if the dogs could locate simple sunken objects.

Pedro felt the excitement fizzing like soda in his chest and pulled a root beer Dum Dum lollipop out of his pocket to suck on. In spite of his intuition telling him that Gem might be the water dog he was looking for and the perfect dog for Laurel Leon, he knew it wasn't a good idea to get his hopes up. Gem's response to water and the weeks and weeks of training ahead would tell him. All he could do was observe. He crunched down on the lollipop and shattered it in one bite.

"Well, at least we've got the place to ourselves," Martin announced when they pulled into the deserted parking lot next to a small lake. "No wait for the ramp!"

Roxanne and the kids unloaded the dogs first. Then Pedro backed the trailer down the boat ramp and he and Martin launched and tied the Zodiac before taking the kayak off the roof rack and parking the vehicle in the lot.

The moment that Captain—a burly black Labrador—saw the lake, he wanted to get in. He whined and pulled at his leash. "Let's let them explore," Roxanne said, giving the okay to turn the dogs loose. Captain raced into the water immediately, undeterred by the fifty-five-degree temperature, and then ran back onto shore to shake, spraying Roxanne and the kids with cold droplets.

Gem hadn't been to a lake before. She walked to the water's edge cautiously, sniffed, and lapped up a bit of lake water. Then she waded in, wagging. Water was fun! She dug at it, splashing herself in the face and sending Juniper into peals of giggles. "You can't dig a hole in the water, Gem!"

Only Sally seemed uneasy, regarding the lake skeptically. Morgan felt for her—she understood that new things weren't always easy. She ran a hand over the reluctant dog's back and came up with a handful of fur—a sure sign of nervousness. "It's okay, Sally," Morgan reassured the spotted dog, coaxing her closer so she could see that water wouldn't hurt her.

Pedro, Roxanne, and Martin stood back, watching the kids and dogs. It was nice to let them discover the area without a strict agenda. Pedro's eyes were glued on Gem, and the flicker of hope inside him was glowing brighter.

When the dogs—even Sally—were comfortable on the shore, Roxanne called them to the Zodiac. She climbed into the big gray-and-yellow rubber-sided boat and stood beside the engine. Then she called each dog, one by one, to get in with her. Captain and Gem both bounded aboard, unfazed by the motion of the boat in the water, and Forrest and Juniper clambered on after them. Sally stood shaking on the beach.

"It's okay," Morgan coaxed her. She got on first and patted her leg. Slowly, a quivering Sally followed. As quickly as she was in the boat, she was back out. Morgan followed the reluctant spaniel, clipped a leash on her, and coaxed Sally back aboard. The lead seemed to make her feel slightly more secure.

With Pedro in the kayak and Martin at the tiller, the crew motored toward deeper water.

The scene from Pedro's seat in the sleek orange kayak was almost comical. He was too far away to hear what everyone was saying, but he could see exactly what was going on. Captain began barking loudly, broadcasting his delight and going from one side of the boat to the other as if deciding where to jump overboard. His excitement was too big to be contained! Sally stayed beside Morgan, and it was clear the girl was working double time to help the dog feel less afraid, petting and talking to her. At the front of the boat, with her nose up and red-gold chest puffed, Gem stood with her two front paws on the prow. She looked proud enough to be a hood ornament!

Martin steered them into a small cove, and Roxanne threw a float for the dogs to retrieve. Captain and Gem jumped fearlessly from the Zodiac.

"Gem's doing the dog paddle!" Juniper shouted, clapping her hands.

Forrest nudged her. "What'd you expect, the backstroke?" Juniper smacked his arm, and Martin quickly intervened before one of his kids ended up in the water with the dogs! The dogs did a few more retrievals, and then, after much effort and a lot of wriggling and hauling, they were back in the boat. With everyone decidedly damp and chilly, they turned back toward the docks. Sally remained curled in the bottom of the Zodiac. She had stopped shaking, but it was clear she'd never venture into the lake. On the way back, they passed a few boats that had launched since they first set out. Captain barked hellos, while Gem wagged her tail like it was the flag on a ship. Poor Sally started shaking all over again when the rocking increased.

"Not for you, huh, Sally?" Morgan stroked her back gently. "That's okay," she said.

Back onshore, Roxanne and Martin yanked the boat up onto the ramp, and Pedro, who had already taken the kayak out of the water, maneuvered the trailer to the edge of the launch. While they secured the crafts, Juniper, Morgan, and Forrest took the pups back to the small beach that, come summer, would be crowded with towels and beach chairs and swimmers, but for now stood empty. Sally's tail had come back up as soon as her paws hit solid ground. Gem was happy to be on the beach, too. She snuffled her nose in the loose pebbly dirt. She pawed at it. This strange soft soil was nice, almost as nice as the water. It would be good to dig in. She could dig way down and make a huge hole filled with all kinds of new smells. But she was so tired! She felt drained and flopped down on the sand while Captain charged back into the lake after a stick.

Juniper plopped onto the dirt beside Gem and reached over to pet her soft head. It had been an exciting day, but she'd never seen Gem too tired to dig. The golden enjoyed a good dirt-flying session more than any dog she'd ever seen. Juniper dug a little with her hand to demonstrate that this was a good spot for digging. Gem closed her eyes.

The golden retriever lay in the sand until it was time to get into the van. Then she hopped in gingerly, curled up, and tucked her nose under her tail.

"Long day?" Pedro asked as he leaned down to give the damp dog a pat.

But Gem was already asleep.

11

Roxanne sat beside Pedro in the passenger seat on the drive back to the ranch. They always appreciated an opportunity to compare notes after training sessions, and Pedro was perpetually amazed at how much more Roxanne noticed during these excursions than he did. Getting away from the ranch brought her already-keen dog senses to an even higher level. Pedro didn't need Roxanne to tell him that Sally wasn't going to work with the Coast Guard, but Pedro thought Captain and Gem both showed clear signs of being great water dogs . . . especially Captain!

"Yep, I'd say he liked it," Roxanne said, grinning. They both knew liking water didn't necessarily mean that a dog would be trained for water rescues. But it *was* something to put on the dog's résumé. It might lead to future training, or it might not.

"And what about Gem?" Pedro asked. Though he admired Captain's exuberance, he liked Gem's calm enthusiasm a little better, at least for the job he had in mind. She didn't have to do water rescues, per se; she just needed to be comfortable in aquatic environments. "You think she'd be okay working near, say, the ocean?"

"Sure. She was stable out there today," Roxanne said, nodding. A slow smile was growing on her face. "I'm getting the feeling you have something in mind. I can see your wheels turning up there . . ." She pointed at Pedro's forehead.

Pedro put a hand on his chest. "Me?" he asked innocently, and then added, "Say, can you pop the glove compartment? I stashed some Skittles in there . . ." Pedro was adept at changing the subject when necessary.

Roxanne got out the candy and poured a few into Pedro's waiting hand. "You know we *just* started training, right? It's going to be a while before Gem's ready for a handler."

"I know, I know." Pedro transferred the Skittles from his hand to his mouth two at a time without looking at them—he liked to guess the flavor combinations. "I'm not in a hurry!" he said with an easy laugh. "I just like to make the right match." Still, he had to admit he couldn't wait to tell Laurel about Gem's potential.

Back at the ranch, there was a lot to do: The trailer had to be unhitched, the Zodiac and kayak had to be hosed off and dried for stowing, the gear had to be toweled and put away, and of course the dogs needed their regular care like always.

Everyone scrambled out of the car in a heap. Morgan and Juniper were on dog detail, while the three adults and Forrest took care of the gear. Morgan took Captain and Sally, who was still sticking close to her side. Juniper watched Gem hopping out with the other dogs, and thought she saw the pup wince. Worry climbed up her spine as she led the dog into the canine pavilion and to her bed. While Morgan prepared food bowls, Juniper lingered by Gem's kennel. She was bunking right beside Captain, and while they both looked worn out from the trip, Gem looked especially beat.

"All that water time wore you out, huh, girl?" she asked, taking Gem's kibble-filled bowl from her sister. Gem gave a slow wag when Juniper set the dish on the floor, but didn't get up from her bed. "Come on, you must be hungry," Juniper encouraged her. It was not at all like Gem to be uninterested in a meal.

Gem stood slowly. Her legs were sore. Her back was sore. *All* of her was sore. She limped over to her bowl and nosed the kibble. She took a few bites, but all she really wanted to do was lie back down. She felt stiff and tired.

Juniper watched Gem the whole time, her eyebrows dipping lower and lower. Something was definitely off. They usually removed the bowls when the pups were done eating, but Juniper left Gem's uneaten food in her kennel when they headed to the house for their own meal.

The Sterling kitchen smelled even better than usual with both dinner *and* early Thanksgiving preparations going on. Juniper smelled the cinnamon stick simmering in the cranberry sauce and detected a bit of orange, too. Layered over that was the smell of pasta carbonara in all of its garlicky, bacony goodness.

Juniper washed her hands and took her seat. She was usually chatty at meals but didn't feel like talking tonight. When the pasta bowl came her way, she took just a small scoop.

Georgia looked at her daughter suspiciously and almost jumped up from her chair to place a hand on her forehead and check for fever. "Are you feeling okay, Juniper?" Though she was the smallest in the house, she ate as much as any of them and sometimes more. The tiny heap of noodles on her plate was unusual. And she hadn't cruised past the stove to see if there was anything she could stick her fingers into on her way to the table, either. Something was wrong.

Juniper shrugged. "Just worried, I guess. Gem didn't want her dinner."

Georgia's already-big brown eyes grew bigger with concern.

"She's probably just tired," Morgan offered. "We had a big day. Or maybe she drank too much lake water. She'll eat when she's ready."

"Yeah," Forrest agreed. He was tired, too, though it wasn't keeping him from shoveling forkfuls of food into his mouth.

"Just seems like she'd be extra hungry." Juniper tried a few bites. She could feel her mom watching her—worried the same way she was—and made an effort to finish everything on her plate. The second she was done with her dish duty, she scooped up Bud and headed back to the pavilion.

The bowl of dog food still sat untouched, and Gem didn't stand up to say hello. Juniper's worry spiked as she sat down inside the kennel next to Gem's bed. She set down Bud and an old favorite book, *Henry and Mudge in Puddle Trouble*, too, and pulled the bowl of food closer. While she read, she offered Gem a few bits of kibble at a time with her free hand. Gem obediently licked and crunched each piece without enthusiasm. Bud, who sat curled between Gem and Juniper, purred loudly.

When the story was finished and the bowl was empty, Juniper stood to go. Bud didn't move—he just gazed up at Juniper and kept on purring. "Okay, Buddy, you stay here and keep an eye on her," Juniper told the cat solemnly.

Gem watched the girl close the gate and walk away. Her stomach clenched. She had eaten the food from Juniper's fingers because the girl had offered it, but now it felt like it wanted to come back up. She ached all over. The warm spot of cat curled beside her was a small comfort. She closed her eyes. And after a long while, she fell asleep.

12

Juniper was up before anyone else in the house. Usually she was the second to last out of bed on weekends and holidays. Fifteen-year-old Shelby, a champion sleeper, was last. Today, though, Juniper slipped out of bed without waking Twig and tiptoed through the quiet house. She yawned as she opened the back door. Maybe she wasn't up early. Maybe she had never really slept!

In the pavilion, most of the dogs were still dozing. For a moment, it looked like Gem was sleeping soundly, but when Juniper got closer, her eyes opened.

Gem thumped her tail when she saw who it was. She got to her feet and walked slowly toward Juniper. Every step hurt, but she kept up her slow wag.

Juniper cringed as she watched the pup struggle forward and hurried to open the kennel. Gem didn't seem like herself. She looked wiped out, and worse, she was definitely limping. All night in bed (while she wasn't sleeping), Juniper had tried to convince herself that Gem was just tired out from the lake trip. And all night she lost the argument in her mind. Now, seeing Gem, it was confirmed. Something was really wrong.

In the kennel beside Gem's, Captain was up and wagging. He stretched his front paws, dipping his head low while his rear end (and flapping tail) stayed high in the air, then scampered over to try to fit his tongue through the fencing to give Juniper a lick. He'd worn himself out the day before, too, but today he seemed fine. It was double confirmation.

Juniper let herself into Gem's enclosure. Bud stretched and came to greet her, and she bent to run her hand over his spine. He arched his back and purred. "Thanks for taking care of my girl," Juniper said as she let him out the kennel door.

She gave Gem a gentle pet on the way back to the dog bed. She patted the pup's sleep cushion. Gem walked over and lowered herself gingerly. Juniper sat beside Gem's bed and stroked her, lightly rubbing her legs. Her chest was tight with worry, and she had to fight back tears. She wasn't sure what to do or who to tell. Luckily, Roxanne walked into the pavilion at that very moment wearing sweatpants, bedhead, and a worried expression.

"Hey, June. What's going on?" Roxanne could immediately tell that neither Gem nor Juniper was herself. They both looked like inner tubes with the air gone out of them. Georgia had texted Roxanne last night, asking if she could please check on Gem this morning so that they could set Juniper's mind at ease. Roxanne knew already that she couldn't declare an all's-well.

"Has she eaten?" Roxanne asked.

Juniper nodded, then shook her head. "I hand-fed her last night. That was the only way I could get her to eat. And I think she's in pain. She's limping."

"Come, Gem!" Roxanne crouched down and called the dog. She didn't want to torture her, but she had to see for herself. Gem got up slowly and walked toward her with a definite hobble.

As Juniper watched, a pair of tears overflowed her eyes and slid down her cheeks.

Gem let Roxanne feel her all over to check for swelling, something that would indicate a strain or sprain or break. Even if she found a swollen limb, it wouldn't necessarily explain the lack of appetite, and she didn't feel anything particularly unusual, anyway. After a few minutes of standing, Gem began to tremble, and Roxanne let her lie back down.

Juniper couldn't hold back any longer. "Does this mean she'll never be a SAR dog?" She let out a ragged sob. She felt so responsible for this dog, for Gem. She had picked her!

Roxanne stopped petting Gem and patted Juniper's back instead. "Let's not panic," she said. Juniper was known to be dramatic, but the tears on her face weren't theatrics; they were tears of genuine concern. "We don't know anything yet. Gem might have just eaten something funny." She was a dog, after all. "Or she might have a virus. It could be anything. I'll call Dr. Jessica. She can help us figure it out."

Roxanne hoped Juniper found some comfort in her words. Meanwhile she was trying to keep her own brain train from going off the rails. Lists of illnesses and their corresponding symptoms flashed through her head—she needed to take her own advice. "Let's not borrow trouble. Right now we need to gather the facts and get a diagnosis."

Dr. Jessica, the ranch's on-call vet, did not pick

up her phone, so Roxanne left her a detailed message. She hung up and began to wonder if she should contact an emergency vet—it being so close to a holiday, Dr. Jessica might be away or . . . She didn't have time to complete the thought. Her phone buzzed, and the veterinarian's name appeared on the screen.

Roxanne walked away from Juniper and Gem to talk to Dr. Jessica privately. They didn't need to hear the details of the situation. Not yet. She explained it all quietly into the phone. The vet's "uh-huhs" and "okays" were soothing.

"I'll be over this afternoon to take a look at her," Dr. Jessica said when Roxanne finished.

They clicked off, and Roxanne shared the news with Juniper. The vet would be by this afternoon. "Until then, she said, Gem should just rest in her kennel, and we will have to wait."

Juniper let out a heavy sigh. Waiting was not her favorite.

🐾 🐾 🐾

Opening the door to his trailer, Pedro took a deep breath. The morning air had a slight crispness to it, and the human trainer wished he were a dog. If he *were*, he'd be able catch a whiff of the pies he was certain were baking down at the Sterling house. He breathed out and smiled. Thanksgiving was one of his favorite holidays, and tomorrow could not come soon enough! Stepping back into his cozy home, Pedro picked up his phone. He located a number and hit call.

"Hello?"

The voice on the other end was friendly and got even friendlier when he said his name.

"Pedro! I've been hoping you would call, but didn't expect to hear from you so soon. You said this could take a long time!"

Pedro laughed. Laurel Leon sounded as he'd expected her to: confident, fun-loving, kind, and surprised. "I know, I know, but listen. The dog I have in mind is just starting her SAR training. It will still be a while before you can even meet her.

I just wanted you to know that I have a great lead."

"That's such good news!" Laurel chirped.

"Don't get your hopes up too high," Pedro said, knowing that she wouldn't be able to help it.

"I know, I know," Laurel echoed back to him. She then repeated what he had already told her twice in email: "We won't know until we know, and in the end it's all up to the dog!"

Pedro hung up feeling good, located his coffee mug, and took a sip. The only thing that would make his favorite morning beverage better was a slice of pumpkin pie! Or maybe apple. He could never decide which he liked more.

His phone interrupted his pastry dreams. "Roxanne!" he answered. He hadn't expected her to call. They were both off today, and Roxanne was supposed to be leaving to visit her sister for the holiday.

"Hey." She sounded glum. "I'm calling about Gem. She's sick." Pedro felt his heart sink while Roxanne explained that she wasn't sure what was wrong, but that Dr. Jessica was coming. "Maybe it's nothing," she said, but her tone spoke volumes. It said she thought it was definitely *something*.

When he ended the call, Pedro stood for a long moment with his phone in his hand. He could dial Laurel's number right now and tell her that the dog he'd just told her about was sick . . . or he could wait. He slid the phone into his pocket. They'd have more info soon. And maybe it really *was* nothing. He hoped so.

13

"Come on, June," Morgan coaxed. "Let's get something to eat. Gem will be fine by herself for a little while."

Gem's tail thumped weakly at the sound of her name. Juniper squeezed her eyes closed and shook her head so hard her braids bobbed. "I can't leave her!" she exclaimed. "I just can't." Morgan thought her little sister was going to burst into tears, but she bit her lower lip, stroked Gem's soft golden back, and held it together.

"You're not helping Gem by not taking care of yourself," Morgan tried. "She wants you to be happy . . . and fed. I'll make you a grilled cheese . . ."

Juniper's tummy grumbled in spite of her desire to stay with Gem. She almost never skipped a meal. She loved food . . . and she *especially* loved Morgan's grilled cheese. She looked up at her sister. "You will? Without crust?"

Morgan nodded. "Of course. We have your favorite cheddar, too. Come on. We can do some online research while we're in the house. We might be able to find out what is going on, and figure out how to help her."

Gem lifted her head and licked Juniper's hand, as if giving her permission to leave. Juniper leaned over and planted a kiss on the pup's head before getting to her feet. "Come on, Bud," she called, patting her hip. But the gray kitten just looked up lazily and leaned back into Gem, arching her neck over one of the dog's front paws. He clearly wasn't going anywhere.

"Okay, Bud. You look after her some more . . .

you're doing a good job," Juniper agreed, as if she'd thought of it herself.

The two girls left the pavilion, and by the time they were halfway to the house, they could smell deliciousness. Georgia was in the kitchen with her long unruly curls tied back and an apron covering her front. She was baking pies for Thanksgiving dessert, and a pot of spiced apple cider simmered on the stove.

"Hi, girls," she said, wiping her hands on her apron. "How's Gem doing?"

"She's really sick," Juniper said, sliding onto a seat at the counter. "We're going to find out what she has after lunch."

"We're going to try," Morgan corrected her. Morgan found a corner of counter space near the stove and gathered the ingredients for the grilled cheese. She buttered two pieces of bread and cut slices from the block of sharp cheddar.

"Ooh, can I get one of those?" Georgia asked. "Pretty please?" She had been in the kitchen all morning but hadn't fed herself a bite. She slid a pumpkin pie into the oven. Then she gave Morgan's shoulder a squeeze in thanks.

When their bellies were filled with toasted bread and cheese and warm spiced cider, Morgan got out the laptop the younger kids shared. "I think we should start with common dog illnesses." She typed in the words and clicked through on "stiffness and pain," which seemed closest to what Gem was dealing with. It was kind of hard to pinpoint because the symptoms had come on suddenly and Gem hadn't lived there very long. Plus, she was a rescue. They didn't know her history other than the medical records that came from the shelter.

Morgan typed "lameness" into the search engine and sighed. "We hardly know·anything about Gem. We don't even know if she's a purebred."

"We know she's purely perfect!" Juniper said. "And why would being a purebred matter?"

"Purebreds are more likely to have genetic issues like arthritis, bad hips, or joint problems," Morgan replied as Twig hopped up onto Juniper's lap with a loud meow.

Juniper's mouth hung open in dismay for several seconds while she stroked Twig's back. Finally she snapped it closed and brightened a little. "Maybe Dr. Jessica can tell us if she's all golden retriever."

Morgan nodded, but she was already on to the next search. She typed in "kennel cough," then deleted it because she knew that Gem had already been vaccinated against that, as had all the dogs on the ranch. In fact, according to the shelter records, Gem was up to date on all her vaccines. And she'd gotten a clean bill of health from Dr. Jessica a couple of days after she arrived on the ranch.

Morgan tapped her fingers on the countertop, thinking. She knew some dog diseases were tricky. They could hide for a long time in the body and then suddenly appear.

She typed "hidden diseases in dogs" and scrolled through the page of search results hoping something would grab her attention. Finally, something did.

"Here!" she said, leaning in so close she blocked Juniper's view. Juniper pulled her back, but instead of reading what was on the screen, she watched her sister's eyes dart back and forth. Morgan's brow was as wrinkly and furrowed as a shar-pei's.

"This could be it . . ." she whispered. "Lyme disease."

Juniper leaned in to read the list of symptoms on the screen: lameness, loss of appetite, lethargy. "What's lethargy?" she asked.

Morgan paused in her reading. "Being tired all the time."

Juniper's eyebrows shot up, and the sisters shared a knowing look. "She has that!" Juniper exclaimed.

Morgan nodded. "She sure does. It doesn't seem like she's been in the woods a lot, but deer and their ticks can be almost anywhere, and the ticks can really make a dog or a person sick . . ."

Juniper felt a little sick herself. Lyme disease looked scary. "I've never found a tick on her," she mumbled after reading how the disease was usually contracted. She blinked back tears. Lyme disease could be fatal!

"I know," Morgan agreed. "But it could have happened before she came here. It says symptoms might not show up for a few weeks." She sighed and closed the computer. "There's no point in worrying, June," she said for both of them. "Dr. Jessica will be able to tell what's going on after she runs some tests. In the meantime, let's go check on our golden girl. I want to see if Sally's recovered from the lake trip, too."

Juniper slid off her stool, suddenly overcome with the desire to see Gem again. She just felt better when they were together. "I'll see you later, Twig," she said, scooching the cat off her lap.

When they got back to the pavilion, Gem was already in the exam room with Dr. Jessica. Morgan leashed up Sally and took her out to the training grounds, while a nervous Juniper scooped up Bud, who was sitting patiently outside the exam room door. The two of them paced, and Juniper fretted. She tried to hold on to hope as tightly as she was holding on to her squirming cat. She and Morgan had to be wrong!

Dr. Jessica emerged just as Roxanne and Morgan and Sally returned. The doctor wasn't smiling, and Juniper squeezed Bud so hard he yowled and leaped to the ground. "Is it Lyme disease?" Juniper blurted.

Dr. Jessica looked surprised for a moment, then gave Juniper a pitying look . . . the kind Juniper hated more than anything. The kind that made her feel like a baby. "That's a very good guess," Dr. Jessica told them all. "But we won't know for sure until I get results back from the lab."

"Will it . . ." Juniper swallowed hard. ". . . kill her?"

Dr. Jessica's expression turned grave, and she inhaled deeply. "Let's wait and see what the results are before we start worrying," she replied.

Juniper felt her stomach tighten. Too late for that.

14

The smell of sautéing onions and mushrooms and celery drifted into Juniper's snoozing nose, making her open her eyes. Her mother was making stuffing! Juniper loved everything about Thanksgiving dinner, but her mother's stuffing was her absolute favorite—she liked it even more than her mom's amazing pumpkin pie or famous lasagna. Her mouth started to water, and then she remembered.

Gem was sick. Gem wasn't going to be feeling thankful today . . . she was going to be feeling awful. Juniper lay in bed feeling awful herself, then began trying to talk herself out of it. Maybe there was some new information . . . maybe Dr. Jessica's test results were in. She threw off the covers and got dressed in a hurry. The pull to find out how Gem was doing was so strong that she almost didn't bother going to the bathroom or brushing her teeth. Almost.

She knew her mother would want her to eat something, so on her dash through the kitchen she announced, "I'll be back in a few!" Georgia did not try to stop her, and Juniper suspected that her mother might know the test results already and could probably tell her, but she wanted to be with Gem when she heard them.

🐾 🐾 🐾

Inside her kennel, Gem could smell Juniper coming. She struggled to get to her feet as the door to the pavilion opened, but her body ached all over and didn't work quite right. It took a long time just to stand up. Her legs wobbled. And the worst part was that the pains and the wobbles kept moving around inside her body. She never knew what was going to hurt.

"Hey, girl," Juniper crooned as she opened the door to the enclosure and watched the pup approach. Gem was limping on her left side, which was different from the day before. She called her back to her bed, sat down beside her, and rested the pup's head in her lap while a displaced Bud groomed himself near Gem's water bowl. "Good dog," Juniper crooned. "Best dog."

"Hey there, Juniper." Roxanne came out of the little office off the main section of the pavilion. She held a bottle of pills in her hand and wore a serious expression as she joined them in Gem's kennel. She took a breath. "Okay, I don't want you to freak out. That won't help anyone." Roxanne placed a hand on Juniper's shoulder, a clear sign that the news was bad. Juniper took a deep breath, too, to steel herself.

"Gem does have Lyme disease."

Juniper shuddered and swallowed a sob.

"That's the bad news. The good news is that there is medicine for Lyme." She shook the bottle in her hand lightly. "She's probably going to be just fine!"

Juniper swallowed back her tears. "Probably?" she croaked out. *"Probably?"* That really didn't seem like enough.

Roxanne pressed her hand into Juniper's shoulder, as if physically trying to ground her. "She needs to take antibiotics for six weeks. They should start to work on her symptoms almost immediately."

"But what about kidney failure and heart damage?" Juniper asked in a panic. She spotted Bud, still grooming himself. He'd spent the last few days snuggled up with Gem. "Is it contagious?" she practically wailed.

Roxanne was beginning to feel out of her Juniper-calming depth when the door to the pavilion opened and Georgia appeared. The mother of four did indeed know what Gem's diagnosis was, and also that the news would hit her youngest hard. Full meltdown mode was, somewhat unfortunately, one of Juniper's go-tos.

"It's Lyme disease!" Juniper cried, jumping up and running to her mom for a hug. Georgia smoothed Juniper's hair and let her cry it out. When her sobs subsided, she tilted Juniper's head upward and looked her in the eye. "I think you are the perfect person to give Gem her medicine," she said. "She knows how much you love her, and it might help her get better."

Juniper wiped the tears from her face and nodded. "Okay," she said. "If you think it will help . . ."

"I think it will definitely help," Georgia confirmed.

Roxanne nodded her agreement. "Your mom needs to get back to making our Thanksgiving feast." The trainer's plans had changed with a sick dog in the house. She was disappointed not to be going to her sister's for the holiday after all, but the Sterling family feast she'd get to attend instead was a delicious consolation prize. "How about I show you how to tuck the pills in peanut butter?"

Juniper sniffled and nodded, following Roxanne over to the kitchen-like area of the pavilion, complete with cupboards. It turned out that the pill wrapping was pretty simple—you just covered the capsule in peanut butter and that was it. She fed the pill to Gem, who actually seemed to enjoy it! Juniper smiled for the first time since she'd arrived in the pavilion that morning. She let the pup—and Bud—lick the remaining peanut butter off her fingers, which tickled.

"Excellent work," Roxanne said, smiling at the threesome. "I know this is hard, Juniper. But we're just going to have to—"

"I know, I know," Juniper interrupted with a heavy sigh. "Be patient," she said before anyone else could say the awful words out loud.

🐾 🐾 🐾

Pedro sat in the skid loader watching Martin lean over the engine, tinkering. The digger had been finicky all fall—slow to turn over and sputtery—and just the other day refused to start altogether. Martin had been working on it a little every day, with Pedro helping out whenever he had time. Martin prided himself on being able to fix things, and was not giving up . . . not even on a holiday.

Pedro admired the way Martin, who had a busy schedule to begin with, jumped in to try to teach himself whatever skills he needed to keep things running at the Sterling Center—and there were a lot of them. From buildings to water to electricity to machinery to landscaping . . . something always needed attention on the ranch, and often many things at once! Martin was a jack-of-all-trades and so good at his behind-the-scenes occupation that his work was almost invisible to others. The ranch was lucky to have him.

"Pedro!" Martin called, and Pedro realized with a jolt that he hadn't been watching for the sign that he should try the engine. He quickly leaned forward and turned the key, which yielded a turn-over but no start.

"Okay, turn it back off," Martin said, wiping his brow and leaning in again. "I've got one more idca."

Pedro went back to his thoughts. He'd been distracted all morning . . . distracted and worried about not telling Laurel that Gem had Lyme disease the second he'd heard the news. He'd been going back and forth in his mind for hours now. Was it worse to keep Laurel's hopes up, or dash them before any of them knew how it was all going to turn out? Gem would have been ready to start training with a handler in a few weeks, and now it would be a month at the bare minimum, maybe more. And that was if she didn't suffer any of the lingering effects of the illness. He just wasn't sure whether keeping it to himself was the right thing or not. He popped a Sour Patch Kid into his mouth and chewed furiously.

"Okay, try again," Martin called.

This time Pedro was ready. He leaned forward and turned the key, listening as the skid loader engine sputtered once and then roared to life. The two men smiled at each other, savoring their moment of success. That was something!

15

Laurel Leon buzzed with energy. She started every day with a run on the beach, but today she felt like she could run forever. She hit her usual six-mile mark and slowed to a walk, and eventually a stop. Shielding her eyes, she looked out at the Pacific Ocean. The water was a steely blue, relatively calm, and glinted in the early morning sunlight. Yes. This morning she had both energy *and* time, and it seemed like an excellent way to start this new chapter of her life.

Smiling to herself, Laurel pulled off her sneakers, stashed her house key inside one toe, and placed them next to the leg of one of the light blue lifeguard stands that dotted the long beach. Taking a breath, she charged into the waves in her running shorts and workout top. When she'd made it past the break, she turned and swam parallel to the shore, kicking and slicing through the salt water with her arms, her long limbs propelling her forward. Laurel loved all kinds of water, but salt water always made her body feel particularly buoyant, almost like she didn't have to do anything to keep herself on the surface. It was a wonderful, freeing floating sensation.

She swam along the shore for a long while, her mind moving as fast as her body. Today was the day she'd leave to meet Pedro Sundal, the Sterling Center staff, and possibly her next four-legged partner. It was all a bit hard to believe.

Just thinking about getting a new partner turned her mind to her last canine companion, her sweet Bluto. Though he'd been gone for almost two years, the enormous Lab-and-Newfoundland mix had been her partner and her best friend for a long time before his unexpected illness. If he were still with her, he would be either swimming a few yards away or watching her from the sand, ready to pull her to safety if he noticed anything amiss. Both Labs and Newfoundlands were well-established water dogs, and Newfoundlands had been known to accompany sailors and fishermen on long sea voyages. There were many tales of the large, well-suited-to-swimming dogs saving men from sinking ships in freezing waters. It was just what they did.

Laurel turned to swim back to her starting point and slowed her stroke. She told herself that this new dog wasn't Bluto, that Bluto was gone and could not be replaced. Comparing *any* dog to him could throw off the process of partnering with a new animal. She turned her head slowly, looking out over the sparkling blue of the ocean, and reminded herself to stay open. The whole reason she'd been without a dog for so long was to give herself time to mourn so she could embrace a new dog and a new relationship.

When she reached her starting point, Laurel put her feet down onto the sand and shuffled out of the water, keeping her feet on the bottom so she wouldn't step on any stingrays that could be hanging out near the shore. She shook out her short, dark curls—rather like a dog—and dripped back to her shoes. As she stood there getting the sand under her feet wet, she realized that she'd forgotten a towel and laughed aloud. She was usually an extremely prepared person! It was one of the characteristics that made her good at her job. Today, though, she clearly had other things on her mind.

She sat on a nearby driftwood log for a few minutes until she wasn't sopping, then let the sun and the breeze dry her the rest of the way on the walk home. After a quick shower, she checked her list, finished packing, and loaded up her Prius for the drive up the coast toward her future.

🐾 🐾 🐾

Georgia walked through the handlers' quarters after lunch on the first day of the new year, making sure everything was ready. It had been a challenging several weeks for her clan, what with holiday activities, Gem being sick, and Martin struggling more than usual with equipment problems. But things had finally settled, and she was looking forward to getting back to a regular routine and the upcoming arrival of some new potential handlers . . . starting this afternoon. She liked it best when the center was full of both dogs and people.

The dorm-like rooms in the handlers' lodge sported clean sheets and towels, and had been vacuumed and dusted. The kitchen had been recently restocked and wiped down. The whole space was comfortable and efficient—more like a home than a hotel. It reminded Georgia of the hostels where she and her friends used to stay when they traveled around Europe as teenagers. She hoped the arriving handlers would experience the same welcoming feeling. She also hoped that the handler Pedro had in mind for Gem, who'd be arriving first, was the right match. Their resident human trainer seemed stressed about it in a way that worried Georgia—Pedro was not anxious by nature.

The door opened, and Georgia's eldest, Shelby, appeared holding an armful of blankets. "Here are the extras you asked for," she said, handing them over. Georgia took them and carried them to a linen closet in the hall. "I have to get back to the office. Grandma is so deep in her crossword puzzle," Shelby chuckled, "I'm not sure she'd notice a ringing phone!"

Georgia smiled. "I'll be over in a minute." Frances, her mother-in-law, was sharp as a tack but had earned the right to be fully retired. Let her lose herself in a crossword! "Have you seen Juniper lately?" Georgia asked before Shelby disappeared out the door.

"I think she's with Gem and Roxanne. They're taking her through some drills."

Georgia nodded. She was a little worried about

Juniper and this next transition . . . about Gem working with someone *else*. She fluffed the couch cushions in the common room, anxious to find a moment to talk to her most dramatic child. Juniper was passionate about everything she did and was more than just bonded to the charismatic golden pup. She was superglued.

By the time she'd finished giving the space her finishing touches and walked to the welcome center, a silver Prius with a young woman inside was pulling into the parking lot. Georgia watched as a tall brunette unfolded herself from behind the wheel, stretched, and took in her surroundings. The new arrival appeared to be fit and no-nonsense, and Georgia liked both qualities right away. But there was something *else* . . . something behind her strong exterior. She looked vulnerable, too. Georgia was the only person on the ranch who could read people as well as Pedro could, and as she watched the woman hoist her backpack, take a breath, and start toward the door of the welcome center, Georgia had another fleeting thought. The young woman looked . . . lonely.

"You must be Laurel," Georgia said, her smile wide as she reached to take the newcomer's hand. Laurel smiled back warmly.

"That's me," she said. After making eye contact with Georgia, her gaze traveled the walls of the room, taking in the pictures and awards. It already felt like she'd landed in the right place. "I've heard so much about your ranch. It's really a dream to come and meet you all and to have a chance to work with your dogs."

"We're excited to have you," Georgia replied. She'd barely gotten the sentence out when her whirling-dervish daughter marched in through the back door and stuck out her hand.

"Juniper Sterling," she announced, unsmiling. "I'll show you where to put your bags."

Georgia raised an eyebrow at Juniper's less-than-warm introduction. Walking over to Shelby, she very quietly suggested that she accompany her littlest sister on her "tour" and try to buffer her brusqueness.

"I'll try," Shelby replied, shaking her head slightly. She had the feeling Juniper would be grilling Ms. Leon on just about everything. It wasn't going to be easy to live up to Juniper Michelle Sterling's standards!

"Thanks, Liebling," Georgia said, turning back to Juniper and Laurel. "Shelby can help show you around," she explained. "I'll catch up with you later."

Juniper nodded but looked less than pleased as her mother went into her office to answer a ringing phone. A moment later, the other line rang.

"Just give me a second to take this call," Shelby said.

Laurel nodded and smiled.

Juniper tapped her foot impatiently. She was perfectly capable of leading a ranch tour without Shelby's help! She let out a puff of air and listened to her sister on the phone, and when it became clear that the call was going to take more than a couple of minutes, she took advantage of the opportunity.

"Let's go and let Shelby catch up," she said, leading Laurel toward the door. "The ranch is so cool! You're going to love it . . ."

16

Gem stretched out on her bed, enjoying an after-noon nap and feeling the renewed strength in her limbs. Lately she had been feeling so much better! Gone were her aches and pains and limps—the horrible feeling of not wanting to do anything. She was working with Roxanne and Juniper and Morgan again, training a little bit every day. Her tail thumped at the happy thought. She never wanted to feel weak and achy again.

Lifting her head off the bed, she got to work licking the gray tabby kitty, who had become her almost-constant kennel companion. She loved the way the small cat's ears tasted like buttered fish. She loved the soothing sound he made when they were curled up together. The rumble filled Gem with the warm feeling she remembered from when she and Lexa would snuggle together in the girl's bed long ago.

Through the time of being sick and feeling awful, Bud's company had helped Gem get through the long, difficult days. It was so nice not to have to lie aching in her kennel by herself. And now that her legs and neck and back didn't hurt and food tasted delicious again (thank goodness—not wanting to eat made her tail hang low), she liked having Bud around just as much.

Bud rolled over onto his back and stretched, opening one eye in a hello to the golden retriever. He let out a single meow and shimmied a little on his back, then arranged himself so that Gem had easy access to his ears.

During the days and weeks of sick, Gem slept a lot and dreamed of digging in soft scented earth. In her dreams she dug and dug, and nobody yelled or told her she was a bad dog. She was free to send the dirt flying. But no matter how deep she burrowed into the earth, she never found what she was digging for.

Gem stopped licking Bud's ears and rested her chin on her own paws. She let out a long exhale. Life on the ranch was good—the best she'd known. There were a lot of people here who made her feel welcome and loved. She had Juniper and Bud and Roxanne and Eloise and all the Sterling kids. She was almost always warm and was always fed and by now her bed smelled like home (and her favorite cat). She adored training and walking and being given peanut butter globs. But still, she dreamed of digging . . . digging for something else.

Another big exhale ruffled Bud's soft fur. Yes, digging for something else. But . . . what?

The door to the pavilion opened, and Gem forgot all about digging dreams while her tail began to thump. Juniper! She got to her feet and stretched low in front and high in back. A good doggy s-t-r-e-t-c-h!

"Who's the best dog?" the girl's lilting voice echoed in the cement-floored building. Gem wondered what was going on. It wasn't time for peanut butter, and they had already done training today. And Juniper sounded different than usual—her voice was higher, and she smelled a little nervous. Plus there were *other* smells drifting into Gem's black-tipped snout, too. Unusual smells. This was a special visit.

Juniper rushed to Gem's kennel, and Gem licked the girl's fingers through the fence. Someone had come in behind the girl. Yes! *That* was where the different scents were coming from. The person, Gem saw, was a grown-up woman. She smelled like salt water and sunscreen and was stopping at every kennel to greet the dogs inside, one at a time. Gem cocked her head and listened to the sound of her voice, which was solid and calm. Juniper was watching her, too, and Gem couldn't quite smell whether Juniper liked her or not.

When she got to Gem's kennel, Gem thumped her tail on the floor while Bud squeezed under the gate and weaved in and out of the woman's legs, purring. Loudly.

Juniper sighed, feeling extremely torn. She didn't want to move over and let this woman meet her Gem. And she also did. And she didn't. And she did.

Laurel waited patiently, sensing that something was going on with her young tour guide. At last Juniper stepped aside. "This is the dog I was telling you about!" she said, trying to sound excited but feeling like she was being ripped in half. She wasn't sure why she brought this lady straight to the canine pavilion. She knew she wasn't supposed to be introducing her to Gem on her own. And yet her feet just tromped this way.

"Matching up people and dogs is what Pedro and Roxanne usually do," she confessed. "Roxanne's the dog trainer. Pedro's the people trainer."

Laurel chuckled at the term "people trainer," but couldn't really deny the fact that human beings could be tricky and often needed training . . .

herself included! "Yes, I've talked to Pedro. He mentioned a dog," Laurel confirmed.

"But of course it's all up to the dog if they like you or not," Juniper continued as if Laurel hadn't said a word. She crossed her arms over her narrow chest and eyed Laurel doubtfully, as if to question her worthiness.

Laurel took a small step back, surprised to be intimidated by this young person. She hadn't been expecting to be raked over the coals by a kid! She turned her gaze back to the golden dog wagging patiently in her enclosure and reached for the latch on the kennel. "May I?" she asked.

Juniper narrowed her eyes even further and huffed a little. She wanted to say no . . . she knew she *should* say no. They weren't even supposed to be in here! The ranch had a whole protocol about handlers meeting dogs. But usually there were several new handlers, and right now there was only Laurel, and her mom and her sister saw her leave the pavilion, and . . .

Juniper took a breath to stop all her thinking. The truth was, she was dying to see how Gem would respond to this lady. "Okay." Juniper gave a nod and scooped up Bud to give herself something to hold while she watched the interaction.

Laurel unlatched the gate and stepped inside the kennel. She knelt down and let Gem sniff her all over and lick her hands. "Hello, Beauty," she crooned. All the dogs she'd seen in the pavilion were standouts, but the unsmiling little girl was right, this one was special.

The pup had eyes the color of an autumn sunset, the kind of eyes a person could get lost in. The desire to please oozed out of her like honey from a honeycomb. Laurel felt the soft fur on her flank. Pedro had said he had a specific dog in mind for her, a dog who worked well on land and in and around water. She hoped this golden girl was the one.

Juniper squeezed Bud and swallowed. This was hard! Both she and Laurel were still gazing at Gem when the door opened and two more Sterling kids came in, arguing. When they saw the crowd in Gem's kennel, they both stopped short.

"Juniper?" Morgan called her sister's name, her voice full of questions.

"What's going on?" Forrest added, clearly surprised, and not in a good way.

Laurel got to her feet and came out of the kennel to introduce herself.

"Guys, this is Laurel," Juniper said.

Laurel shook hands with the newcomers.

"This is Morgan and this is Forrest," Juniper said without enthusiasm.

If the family resemblance hadn't made the kids' relationship clear, the tension between them did— the air almost crackled with it. Both Morgan and Forrest were looking at their little sister like she was off her rocker.

"Where is Pedro?" Forrest asked pointedly.

"Or Roxanne?" Morgan emphasized the last syllable of the lead trainer's name.

Laurel was beginning to sense that she and Juniper might both be in trouble, but Juniper ignored her older siblings as effectively as an aloof cat. "How should I know? I'm not in charge of them . . ."

Sighing, Morgan and Forrest exchanged a "this is going to be interesting" look.

"Nice to meet you," they said, almost in unison, before getting to work caring for the dogs.

Laurel wasn't sure what was next, but when she turned back to Juniper, the girl was tapping her foot on the floor and eyeing her with suspicion all over again. "Do you know how much kibble a fifty-pound dog should get?" she asked. Laurel was about to answer, but the girl didn't give her the chance. "Two cups per meal. It's not good to over-feed a dog. You may think you're giving them a treat, but it can take years off their life by forcing them to carry around extra weight, which is hard on their organs and joints."

Laurel blinked. "Hey, I'm not the enemy here,"

she replied to the overprotective kid. "I'm all about dogs and what's best for them. I've had a SAR dog before. I know what I'm doing."

"Before?" Juniper echoed. "Why don't you have a SAR dog *now*?"

Laurel felt her brow furrow as a wash of sad memories flooded her mind, followed by a flash of resentment. Who was this kid? Her personal history with dogs was just that . . . personal.

Morgan, who'd been listening in, took a step toward the two of them to try to play the peacemaker, when thankfully the pavilion door opened and Roxanne came in with Captain.

"Oh, hello!" she said, caught off guard. Captain was excited by the presence of a new person and wiggled his back end as he waited for permission to get closer. "I'm Roxanne Valentine, and this big guy is Captain." Roxanne let the dog greet Laurel and then put him in his kennel before shaking the woman's hand. "We've just finished our afternoon training session. I didn't know you'd arrived!"

She raised an eyebrow at Juniper but said nothing. "When the dogs are fed, you three can head off to dinner," Roxanne told the kids in a voice that let them know it wasn't a request. She smiled at Laurel. "I'll take you to meet Pedro, then you can get settled. You must be tired after your drive."

Reeling a little, Laurel just nodded. She gave Gem one last look and followed Roxanne out the door. She felt Juniper's eyes on her back. No doubt the girl wished they were lasers.

17

"You haven't told her?" The exasperation in Roxanne's voice was unmistakable. Pedro felt it as much as he heard it and in a way it was almost a relief, because he'd been feeling exasperated with himself, too.

"No, I haven't. And to tell you the truth I'm not sure why," he confessed. He leaned back against the counter where they prepared the dogs' food and gave Roxanne a sheepish look. "I guess I just wanted Laurel to come and give Gem a chance—"

"Without knowing she has Lyme disease? I mean, that's a pretty big complication to pull out after she's driven halfway up the coast of California."

Pedro shoved his hands in his pockets and rooted around for a piece of forgotten candy. All he found was a wrapper, which he crumpled into a tight ball. He couldn't even look at Roxanne. He felt like a kid disappointing his parents—a kid in trouble. Roxanne wasn't his superior, though. She was his partner and good friend . . . which made disappointing her even worse.

"You could have mentioned it on the phone or in email." Roxanne sounded more baffled than angry. She was trying to understand.

"I know." Pedro's shoulders rose in a feeble shrug.

Roxanne turned and leaned an elbow on the counter beside him. "You know Lyme disease can recur, right? It can cause problems with the heart and kidneys down the line if it flares up. You don't want a handler going into this without full and complete disclosure about the dog . . ." She trailed off. She wasn't sure why she was telling Pedro this—it was stuff he already knew. "The good news is Gem is doing great. The bad news is that doing great is not a guarantee. And now, thanks to an accidental oversight and Juniper being, well, Juniper, she's already met Gem."

Pedro nodded, and Roxanne put her hand on his shoulder. She could tell by his hangdog face that he was already feeling terrible about the situation. He was the one who'd initially lectured her about the importance of entering into a canine partnership with eyes open, with all the critical information revealed to everyone involved. A dog's health clearly fell under "critical."

Roxanne couldn't help blaming herself in part for the predicament. Most training operations would have ruled Gem out as soon as she was diagnosed, but that wasn't the choice that she had made. She'd also let an insistent, spunky nine-year-old participate in training her.

"I thought it would be easier to tell Laurel what

the situation is after she met Gem, though it's certainly not feeling that way now."

Roxanne nodded. She got it. It wasn't always easy to do what they did. They invested so much in the dogs and people they trained. They created heroes. The expectations were high. And hopes were high, too. On top of which, they were all human, and humans were notorious for making mistakes.

"I'll tell her, though. The next time I talk to her on my own, I'll tell her everything," Pedro said. And, he realized, he meant it. Now that Roxanne knew the truth, he had little choice.

Turning, Roxanne opened her arms wide to her friend. There was no sense in piling on! She squeezed him in a hug, and he squeezed back. She knew he would do the right thing.

🐾 🐾 🐾

If *anyone* had told her two months ago that there was *anything* good about getting up at the crack of dawn, Juniper probably would have told that person to get their head examined. But after getting used to her early morning check-ins with Gem, Juniper had discovered that she actually liked the calm moments before the rest of the world was up. The ranch was almost always a busy, noisy place. Only in this pre-alarm time, when the light from the rising sun was still rosy and the air from the fading night was still chilly, was there a reliable quiet. There were no motors or barks or pinging cell phones. It felt like a time that was all her own. Well, hers and Gem's and Bud's.

"Good morning," she whispered as she stepped into the pavilion. She spoke softly so she wouldn't wake the other dogs, or Bud, who did not share her feelings about dawn. Gem was usually awake and waiting, and would wag quietly as soon as she saw Juniper.

"Good morning," a voice answered back.

Juniper blinked in the dim light and stopped where she stood. Laurel was not only in the pavil-ion, she was in Gem's kennel, sitting on the dog bed and petting Gem. *Her* Gem!

"You're up early," Laurel said, a little louder. Her voice was friendly, but Juniper didn't feel much like making friends.

She stared at the athletic woman cradling her favorite dog as the scowl on her face deepened. Gem wagged, waiting for Juniper to come say her hellos, but instead she turned and walked straight to the food counter. She banged the bowls and measuring cup and kibble around, not waiting for Morgan's help like she usually did. She felt mad. Put out. Invaded. Gem was *her* dog!

Except . . . Gem was *not* her dog.

In a sudden flash, Juniper understood why Morgan, her always-perfect sister, often got mopey for several days each time one of her favorite dogs left the ranch with a handler. She always claimed she was really and truly happy for the new teams. And Juniper believed that she was, but could see now how a dog leaving could really put you in a funk. It was hard not to get attached. No, not hard. It was *impossible*.

Juniper took the lid off the peanut butter and tucked in Gem's pill. She carried the coated medicine along with the food bowl over to the open kennel. Gem got up to say hello and sat waiting expectantly for her medicine. She accepted it like a treat and then dug into her breakfast.

Laurel stood up, and they both watched Gem eat. "What was that you gave her in the peanut butter? Fish oil? Is that why her coat is so glossy?" she asked. She hadn't stopped smiling since Juniper came into the pavilion.

Juniper could tell the handler was trying to make conversation—to be friendly. But she still wasn't having it.

"It's medicine. For Lyme disease," she said. "Gem was really sick, you know. She almost died." The words were out of Juniper's mouth before she could think them through. Part of her wanted Laurel, who was obviously smitten with Gem, to partner with the rosy golden and give Gem a great life. And part of her wanted Laurel to just go away.

But now that the words had been spoken, Juniper wished she'd kept them inside. She wished she could snatch them back. And judging by the look on the older woman's face, Laurel did, too. The forced smile was gone.

"I . . . I was just stopping by before my morning run," she stammered.

Juniper suddenly noticed that Laurel was dressed in running shorts and shoes. She bounced lightly on her toes. She looked like she was searching for something else to say but not finding it. After a few awkward seconds, she turned and hurried out of the pavilion.

Juniper's chest felt like someone was hugging her too tight. She felt afraid. She'd already gotten a stern talking-to for introducing Laurel and Gem, and now her angry tongue might have messed things up even more. And for Gem! She looked into the pup's eyes. There was nothing in them but forgiveness. Juniper tried to swallow the lump in her throat. Somehow Gem's unconditional love made it all worse.

18

Laurel stretched briefly outside the pavilion. She'd wanted to take Gem with her on her morning run, but that idea had been quickly scrapped. She wasn't sure what to make of what Juniper had just told her. The girl was like a moody cat—friendly and purring happily on your lap one moment, and then suddenly turning and biting your hand. Still, the news that Gem had Lyme disease hit Laurel hard and put everything into question. Except her run.

Laurel didn't need a dog to go for a run. She'd been running without one for nearly two years now. No dog. No problem. No dog. No problem. She let the words repeat in her head, let them match the rhythm of her pounding feet. She told herself that life without a dog would be easier. It *was* easier. But the thought of continuing to live without a dog made her feel hot behind the eyes. She blinked and picked up her pace, crunching up a small path that led to the outer edges of the ranch.

Laurel tried to focus on her feet and moving forward, but after what Juniper had told her, all the worries she thought she'd put behind her were waiting to meet her right here on the trail: Dogs didn't live as long as humans, the future was always uncertain, goodbye was always inevitable. And the truth was, no matter how long a dog lived, the end came too soon.

An image of Bluto appeared in her mind along with a lump in her throat. He had been taken from her too young. And Lyme disease! She wasn't sure she could handle the complications that might entail, or the potentially shortened life. Not again.

She continued up the trail, turning left when she came to a split. A large Greyhound bus lying on its side loomed in the distance. The ranch was full of surprises. The facility was expansive, and the Sterlings went the extra mile to make sure there were realistic training areas for all kinds of disaster scenarios. She'd seen the destroyed buildings made to resemble a town hit by a tornado or earthquake, and the airplane fuselage. The sites were haunting and impressive all at once.

After passing the bus she spotted another structure that hadn't been on her tour—a trailer. It wasn't spooky in the least, however . . . it was downright homey! The small mobile home was sturdy and tucked into the California landscape. It was neither abandoned nor destroyed. It looked as though it had been planted there like the tidy rosemary and oleander bushes lining the attached porch. As she admired the brightly colored curtains in the windows, she saw one move, and a moment later Pedro opened the front door and stepped out onto the porch.

"Laurel!" he called.

Laurel smiled and came closer. A little out of breath, she put up her hand in greeting.

Pedro waved back. His hair was still messy from sleep, and he was wearing sweatpants and a loose T-shirt. "I don't want to interrupt your run," he told her.

Pedro started to motion her on, but Laurel shook her head and jogged up to the steps. This was her opportunity to tell him that she'd changed her mind, and she wanted to get the news off her chest. She wasn't ready for another canine partner.

"I need to tell you something," the two of them blurted in unison.

"Jinx," Pedro said, still smiling but looking a little confused.

"You go first," Laurel offered. Her breathing

slowed, and she took a seat on the steps and let the breeze cool her sweaty face. Pedro was holding a coffee mug and offered her some, but she shook her head.

After taking a seat beside her on the steps, Pedro spoke the words he'd been avoiding for so long, "Gem has Lyme disease."

Laurel nodded. "I know."

"You do?"

"I just found out," Laurel replied.

Pedro hesitated, then took an educated guess. "Juniper?" he asked, suspecting that he already knew the answer.

Laurel nodded again.

"I'm sorry I didn't tell you sooner. I've known for over a month. But I wasn't trying to trick you. She's a good dog and doing well. She's responded to the antibiotic treatment, and Dr. Jessica says she doesn't think she'll have long-term symptoms. That's not a guarantee, of course. We have no way of knowing if the disease will flare again. But I'm telling the truth when I say I wouldn't have let you come up here if I thought she'd be a bad partner. And she's not the only dog."

Laurel nodded more slowly this time, though her breath was starting to come faster again. She felt unsure . . . about everything. And in her mind Gem *was* the only dog—at least the only one she'd been considering. "When Juniper told me, it made me think that maybe I'm not ready, that maybe I shouldn't have come."

Pedro's face caved in on itself. He quickly hid his devastated expression in his coffee cup. After a long, sweet gulp, he looked up. He had no one to blame for this situation but himself.

"I don't want to push you," he said honestly. "You know I think it's important to be ready for a partnership like this. It's a commitment, and one you have to willingly make. But . . . would you consider giving us a little time before you make your decision? Say, three days?"

Laurel inhaled and closed her eyes, letting the

air out in a rush. "Three days," she repeated, trying to bring some logic into the equation. She was already here, on the ranch. She'd made the trip, and her time off was scheduled. Even if she didn't take the dog . . . She checked her watch to see how much she'd run so far—just one mile. "Let me think about this for about five miles." She smiled weakly at Pedro, got to her feet, and with a little wave was headed up the trail again.

Pedro finger-combed his bedhead and watched her go. His stomach gurgled, filled as it was with coffee and regret. At least she hadn't given him a flat-out no.

19

After running five more miles, Laurel still wasn't sure how she felt, so she ran another three. After running nine miles she was tired. She was sweaty. And she was still torn. She did a bit of stretching outside the handlers' lodge, and then showered and dressed. When she emerged from her room and made her way to the communal kitchen, Pedro was there. He'd showered, too, and looked at her with the kind of hopeful expression she was used to seeing in a dog waiting for another toss of a ball. It was enough to tip the scale.

"Okay. Three days," she said. "I'm all in for three more days. Then we'll see."

The smile on Pedro's face was huge, and Laurel held up her palm to shield herself from the brightness. "I'm not making any promises," she said, warning him away from getting too happy too fast. "This is *not* a promise!" she repeated, trying to convince herself as much as she was trying to convince Pedro.

"We're just asking for a chance," Pedro answered innocently, "and a training session or two." He winked.

Pedro went about the rest of his day feeling relieved. By afternoon, when it was time for Gem and Laurel to train, his relief felt like elation. Roxanne, Forrest, and Morgan were all waiting in the pavilion with Gem, who was in great happy, waggy form. Her coat and eyes sparkled, and she looked more ready than ever to get to work! Nobody would ever guess that this dog had been sick.

Laurel, on the other hand, looked nervous. Pedro gave her a reassuring smile. He knew she wouldn't back out of her agreement to give him three days. He also knew her mind was not made up.

"Where's Juniper?" Laurel asked. Gem wagged harder as she got closer and Laurel knelt down to greet her.

"I was just wondering that myself," Morgan said. Juniper knew the schedule and it wasn't like her to miss *anything* Gem was involved in.

"Maybe she thinks she doesn't have to assist anymore. You know, with you here," Forrest said, looking at Laurel.

"Or maybe the thought of Gem leaving with someone else is just too sad for her to handle . . ." Morgan added.

There was a long moment of quiet. Roxanne frowned at the floor. She knew Forrest and Morgan were probably both right, but it didn't stop her from feeling a little disappointed in Juniper. She'd been doing extremely well, holding up more than her end of the training commitment . . . until now.

"Okay, let's go," Roxanne said. They couldn't let a willful fourth grader stop Gem's progress. The golden was a true standout. She was such a quick learner that Lyme disease had barely slowed her progress. Roxanne thought she might be ready for certification as early as this summer.

"Everyone ready to head out?" Roxanne asked. The sunlight in winter didn't last too long, so they only had a couple of hours to work. The group turned to the door just as it burst open.

"Sorry I'm late!" Juniper charged into the pavilion looking more like her determined self than she had in a while. "I was on the phone with Bud's new agent!" she continued before anyone could even say hello. "And the guy is a serious talker!" She shot them all a "you know the type" expression.

Laurel looked back at her, clearly baffled. "Your cat has an agent?" she asked. Juniper was confusing, to be sure, but this?

"My cats are promising movie stars," Juniper explained, lifting her chin a little higher. "I had almost given up on their careers because it took so long for them to be discovered on YouTube. But Mr. Chance says they want to use Bud in a cat food commercial!"

Laurel still wasn't sure what to make of what Juniper was saying. She looked at the others, who wore expressions ranging from dumbfounded to amused.

"We're still negotiating, however," she continued. "I don't like the terms. They want to pay him in cat food! I told Mr. Chancy Pants they'd have to make us a better offer if they want us to even consider it. I mean, Meow Chow isn't even organic!" She finished by crossing her arms and looking seriously offended.

Pedro laughed first, and everyone else joined in . . . including Juniper.

"Well, we're glad you could take time away from your clients to join us," Roxanne teased. "As it is, we're burning daylight."

"Right!" Juniper rushed over to the wall and grabbed a red leash, handing it over to Laurel. "Red is Gem's favorite color," she said knowingly.

Forrest and Morgan bit their lips together to keep from laughing and exchanged looks with the adults, making a silent commitment not to tell Juniper that dogs were partially color-blind. They could see blue, yellow, and gray . . . but not red.

🐾 🐾 🐾

Because Laurel was already a certified SAR handler, and because he didn't want to pour on the pressure, Pedro sat back to observe the session. Roxanne also took a step back so she could watch how Gem responded with someone new giving the commands. Some dogs didn't like to take commands from different people—they wanted to respond to a single alpha leader. Gem didn't flinch at the switch.

From the moment Roxanne passed the lead to Laurel, Gem gave the ranger her full attention. She was eager to please and wanted to get everything right for the lady who smelled like sunscreen and sunshine.

Roxanne suggested they start with obstacle training, while she gave instructions to Juniper.

Laurel led Gem to the side of the field. There were several contraptions set up along the edge designed to help dogs with trust, balance, and climbing. She clipped off the lead and asked Gem to hop up onto a length of cyclone fencing balanced on cinder blocks. Many dogs refused to walk on grates or fencing or ladders—anything they could see through—because it scared them and messed with their sense of balance.

Gem jumped up and landed gracefully. She didn't like the way the wiry metal felt under her feet— sharp and bouncy at the same time. She would have liked to jump down onto the grass but didn't. Laurel called to her from the other end, and she took one . . . two cautious steps and then strode bravely across. When she reached the other side, she waited patiently for Laurel to invite her to dismount.

"Good dog." Laurel praised the golden when she hopped down to stand beside her on the grass. She gave Gem a small treat from the pouch in her pocket and a good rub around the scruff of her neck. Gem savored it all until it was time for the next obstacle.

Watching from the sidelines, Roxanne and Pedro didn't even have to speak. They just looked at each other while their raised eyebrows said the rest. So far this was a great match!

"Let's try a search," Roxanne called out. She walked over to the practicing team and handed Laurel one of Juniper's socks. Laurel gave Gem a good whiff and then the command the dog had been practicing with the Sterling team.

"Find!"

Gem took a moment to smell the air and locate Juniper's trail. The scent didn't lead her on a direct path to the rubble pile, but Gem diligently followed where it led. She was intent on her target no matter how many twists the trail took, particularly because she was looking for her best cat-scented girl! When she arrived at the foot of the rubble pile—a football-field-sized mountain of debris—she was undeterred. Gem loved the rubble pile. It was big and full of smells . . . and holes that reminded her of digging. It was always an adventure because every step was unsure. She had to think about where she placed her paws and use caution and balance, adjusting almost constantly. It made the search challenging, and finding her target extra rewarding!

Gem wanted to show the sunshine lady she could do it. She liked the sunshine lady. Laurel reminded Gem of Roxanne and made her feel warm. She liked it when she said "good dog" and gave her treats. She liked it when she sat with her on her bed. And when she looked into her eyes.

Gem glanced back to make sure Laurel was watching, letting her know she was ready. Laurel saw her, nodded, and Gem climbed up onto the broken concrete and rebar.

From atop the pile, Gem could smell new things . . . scents were blowing in from far away. More smells wafted up from the tangle of rubble, making the damp tip of her dark nose quiver. Gem stopped and stood completely still. Yes. She smelled exactly what she was after. Placing her feet carefully, she made her way over to the spot and let out a bark. "Woof!" she told Laurel and the others. She'd found the girl! Juniper was here!

Juniper popped up out of a hollow covered in construction dust and let out a sneeze. "Finally!" she yelled. "It's filthy in here!" She waited for Laurel to get as close to them as possible before giving Gem her liver treat reward. Then she and Gem carefully climbed off the trash heap and had a good game of tug with Gem's favorite toy.

Laurel watched the pair, and especially the retriever, with a mixed heart. Gem had done really well. She was a great dog, and the two of them had clicked—it was an undeniable fact. In her rational mind, she knew that the session had gone perfectly.

She knew that this dog was special—smart and loyal and strong and ridiculously talented. She loved her already. But she wasn't sure *she* was strong enough to handle the heartbreak of not being able to work with her if the Lyme disease flared, or worse.

Juniper broke off the game and walked over to the spot where Laurel was lost in thought. "Got my sock?" she asked, holding up one leg and showing the bare ankle over her Converse.

Laurel smiled and pulled the striped sock out of her pocket and handed it over. This was the friendliest Juniper had been since the day she arrived. But the girl's positive demeanor didn't keep the lump from growing in the pit of Laurel's stomach. With less than three days to decide, she remained utterly uncertain.

20

Juniper kicked at the covers that were tying her legs up in knots. The twisted blankets matched the knots in her stomach and made her feel trapped, and frustrated, and wide-awake. Twig opened an eye and glared at his thrashing girl. "Sorry," Juniper said in a not-sorry voice. "At least you can sleep," she groused. She placed her untangled feet on the ground and pushed back the sleep bonnet that had slid down to cover one eye. She knew what she had to do. Moving as quietly as one of her favorite felines, she took her sleeping bag off the top shelf of her closet.

"It's all yours," she whispered to Twig. The tabby was already stretching out to take full advantage of having the twin bed to himself. "Enjoy!" She deposited a quick kiss on his ear. He really was the best orange cat ever. But Juniper had other things on her mind.

She padded down the stairs and out the back door, letting it click shut behind her. With her arms wrapped tightly around her sleeping bag, she ran through the darkness to the canine pavilion.

When the door hinge squeaked, Gem's ears stood at attention. Her tail thumped. She already knew who was coming to see her.

"Hey, girl," Juniper whispered. She didn't want to get the others dogs riled up. She tiptoed to Gem's kennel, unlatched the door, and spread her sleeping bag on the floor. She hadn't brought a pillow. She hadn't forgotten one, either. Gem made a perfect cushion for her head.

"Mrow," Bud complained at having to share the warm cozy spot beside Gem, but it didn't take long for him to curl between his favorite dog and his favorite girl and start buzzing like Martin's electric razor, steady and low. Gem's breathing deepened and so did Juniper's. She yawned as the knots in her belly untied themselves. And then she slept.

🐾 🐾 🐾

In the handlers' lodge, Laurel tossed and turned. She wasn't sure if she'd slept for more than fifteen minutes at a time all night, or the two nights before that! The third of the three days of consideration she'd promised to Pedro had come and gone. Everyone would be expecting her decision in a few hours. She opened one eye, only a sliver. It was morning already. Just barely.

Laurel groaned and sat up. Maybe a run would help her figure out what she was going to do next. Lying in bed not sleeping certainly wasn't! After pulling on some leggings and two layers of sport tops and lacing her shoes, Laurel headed out. It was foggy, and she chose the trail with the steepest incline, determined to sweat out a decision, or perhaps to punish herself for not already knowing. At the peak she paused, her lungs pumping like bellows, and looked down at the gentle valley. A low-lying mist lingered, dipping into the tops of the tallest trees and obscuring the view of the ranch below. She took an extra-deep breath and let it out as slowly as she could.

Training sessions with Gem had been near perfect for three days. Working with the rosy-shaded golden was pure pleasure. Pedro and Roxanne had both told her quietly that she and Gem were a match made in heaven. "What am I so afraid of?" Laurel asked the silence.

The sound of her words faded, and Laurel laughed. She wasn't expecting a voice to answer back, but in a way she *had* been waiting for the answer to appear in some form or another. She just wanted to be sure. It was time to make the decision, and she had absolutely no clarity about her future with or without Gem.

Laurel ran back down from her perch,

descending into the fog. Lost as she was in her thoughts, she was surprised when she arrived at the canine pavilion. Her feet had carried her where her heart was afraid to go. It was still very, very early . . . early enough that she might be able to spend some time alone with Gem. If she couldn't find the answer within herself, maybe the dog could tell her . . . somehow. Hadn't Pedro told her that every canine and human partnership was ultimately up to the dog?

She walked in on cat feet. Tiptoeing closer, she saw that Gem was not alone. Juniper's dozing head was resting on Gem's shoulder, and a smaller gray lump was curled between them, all facing away from the kennel gate. She stood silently watching them breathe in unison for a few moments. The sleeping heap was adorable and squeezed Laurel's heart.

Slowly, Gem's tail started to thump, but she didn't move her head. She knew Laurel was there. Juniper stirred, too. She nestled her face deeper into Gem's ruff, then sat up and stretched. "Hate to say it, Gem, but your bed is not as comfortable as mine! Good pillow, though." She yawned.

Bud stirred next. He stood, stretched, and quickly resettled.

Gem turned her head. She looked right at Laurel and wagged faster. Laurel took two steps back. She didn't want Juniper to see her. She sent a silent thought to Gem, asking the dog not to give her away.

Luckily, Juniper thought the wag was for her and didn't turn to look. She snuggled back down, putting an arm around the fluffy dog. "I'm so glad I found you," she said. "Even if I only got to have you for a little while," she added softly.

Laurel strained to hear.

Juniper readjusted, lying on her side so she could stroke Gem's soft, floppy ear. "You know I don't want you to go, but Mom and Dad have rules about us keeping dogs. We'd be overrun if we adopted every dog. Sure, you're special, but I think

Laurel is probably special, too." Juniper sighed. It hadn't been easy for her to admit that. "She might be almost as good as you are, and I know you'll be happy with her." Laurel thought she heard Juniper sniff. Juniper was quiet for a few seconds before going on. "Besides, my cats need me. I mean, somebody has to look out for their rights. Honestly, you've kind of been a distraction. It's time for me to focus on Bud's and Twig's movie careers . . ."

Laurel fought back a giggle. Juniper was one unique girl! And though she had to strain to make out all her words, it was also as if Juniper were shouting in her ear. Without making a sound, Laurel began to back the rest of the way out.

Gem turned her head, and she and Laurel locked eyes again. Laurel nodded. They didn't need words.

Outside, the fog had cleared, and so had Laurel's clouded mind. As the sun warmed the earth with a rosy glow, Laurel felt better than she had since she'd arrived. She remembered that day, the grilling she'd gotten from Juniper. She understood why now. Juniper hadn't wanted Gem to leave. It wasn't about her at all—it was about the special pup.

She understood how the kid felt, probably better than Juniper would ever know. And what Juniper had said about only having Gem for a little while reminded her that she wouldn't have given up a single second with Bluto, even now, knowing how it all ended. The same would be true of Gem, no matter what happened or how long they had together. Life didn't come with guarantees. Maybe the Lyme would come back. Maybe it wouldn't. It didn't really matter. Either way, Laurel was sure now: Gem was the dog—and SAR partner—for her.

21

Gem wagged and wagged at the small group of people in the Sterling Center parking lot. The door to the car she would soon be traveling in sat open, but she wasn't ready to get into the passenger seat. Not even close!

She and Laurel had worked hard at training every day for the past week. Gem loved the clarity of her handler's directions, the actual searching, and the praise the humans always offered in the form of treats, pets, and games of tug. And now Gem had a *lot* of goodbye licks to give before she and Laurel drove away.

Martin and Georgia and Morgan and Forrest and Shelby all gathered around, a tangle of human arms and legs as they crowded in to stroke her fur. Gem licked each and every one of them in turn, thanking them and wordlessly letting them know that she hoped she'd see them again.

Roxanne was next, and stepped out of the cluster of Sterlings and Pedro to crouch down and look steadily into Gem's eyes. "There's nothing stopping you, Gem," she said. "You will be an official SAR dog before you know it. The rescue world awaits." Gem gave her a big lick right on the cheek and then leaned her head down to nose the little ball of gray fur who'd been weaving in and out of her front legs . . . her kennel companion, Bud. Bud stopped weaving long enough to nose Gem back, then licked the dog's damp snout with her rough pink tongue. All around them, a loud chorus of human "Awwwwwwws" drifted in the chilly air.

With no warning, Juniper sniffed loudly and hurled herself forward, landing on her bottom in front of her favorite dog and one of her favorite cats. She threw an arm around each, squeezing their three heads together. She sniffled as tears sprang from her eyes and ran down her cheeks. They were happy tears, in a way, but also sad.

Martin watched his youngest, his heart swelling. He pulled a rumpled but clean tissue from his pocket and held it out to her. She took it, wiped her eyes, and turned full on toward Gem. Juniper leaned in until their foreheads touched and whispered something so softly into the dog's floppy golden ear that nobody heard what it was. Martin and Georgia exchanged a surprised look, which soon extended to the rest of the group. Juniper was many things, but quiet was definitely not one of them.

When Juniper pulled back, Gem felt something tug at her insides. She was sad to leave Juniper and the purr-motor Bud. All the people on the ranch had been good to her, but these two had *really* made her life better! Her tail thumped on the ground at the thought of seeing them in the future . . . she hoped it would happen before too long. With a final wag, she hopped up into the passenger seat of Laurel's Prius and took a seat with a forward view out the windshield. Laurel smelled like good things and good places from the moment she'd arrived on the ranch, and Gem couldn't wait to see where they were going!

"Looks like she's ready!" Pedro said with a laugh. Laurel nodded, feeling ready and also not ready herself. She went around the circle hugging everyone goodbye and getting squeezes in return. By the time she got to Pedro, her eyes were glistening.

"Thank you so much for matching me with this glorious dog," she said. "And for your patience with me and my decision-making process." The corner of her mouth rose in a crooked smile.

Pedro stroked his salt-and-pepper goatee and smiled back. "Thank *you*," he replied, "for giving our golden girl a shot. And you certainly exhibited some patience of your own . . ." he finished with a chuckle. He reached out his arms, and they hugged. After that, there was just one ranch member remaining.

Laurel turned to the youngest Sterling, who was standing next to the open car door still looking a little teary.

"Thank you for everything, Juniper," she said. "I'm not going to lie—you were a force to be reckoned with. But I'm honored that you trust me to take care of Gem."

Juniper nodded, then raised her head toward the tall woman. "If you think I was tough on you, you should see me with Bud's agent!" Her lips spread outward into a grin, and she rose up on tippy-toe and threw her arms around Laurel's neck. "I just know you'll take good care of her!"

Laurel choked up a bit. "I absolutely will," she vowed. They smiled at each other through their glistening eyes for a long moment, and then Laurel walked around the back of the car, closed the trunk, and climbed behind the wheel.

"Goodbye!" the Sterling clan called as they

pulled out of the parking lot. "Stay in touch!" Gem leaned toward her partially open window and let out a series of goodbye barks. Then with a final honk, they were off.

"The drive is about four hours," Laurel said as they turned onto the two-lane highway a few minutes later. "We'll stop halfway to take a break and give our legs a good stretch."

Gem had no idea what she was saying, but liked the view out the windshield. She liked the way the houses and cars and trees and fences whizzed by. After a while she stuck her head out the window and let her tongue loll, her eyes blinking in the wind. Her heart was filled with happiness. She hadn't been left behind this time. For the second time in a row, she was the one being taken somewhere new by someone she loved. By Laurel! Laurel, who was always clear with commands and quick with praise. Laurel, who smelled like salt water and sunscreen and sunshine.

Laurel, who made Gem feel happy . . . and safe.

22

The drive didn't feel long. Laurel kept her promise, and Gem was still sitting up and taking in all the sights when the Prius pulled off the highway and rolled to a stop in a small parking lot. A minute later Laurel was opening the passenger-side door for Gem.

"How about a little leg stretch?" she said.

She didn't have to ask twice. Once out of the car, Gem's nose quivered madly. The whole area smelled like pee . . . human, dog, and a few other kinds, too! Laurel led Gem to the edge of the pavement where a path meandered into a scrubby forest. Patting her thigh with her palm, she started to jog at a mellow pace. Gem followed along behind, sniffing the air and eventually adding to the smells that permeated the area. Back at the car, Laurel poured Gem a small bowl of water, which Gem lapped up happily. Then it was time to get back on the road.

When they arrived at Laurel's little house in Carpinteria, a small town near the ocean, the sun was already low in the sky. "This is it, Gemmy," she said as she once again opened the passenger door for the pup, then went to the back to unload their stuff.

Gem bounded up the four short steps to the house and waited patiently for Laurel to catch up. Laurel unlocked the door and held it wide. Inside, Gem immediately got to work checking the place out with her nose. The house was a cozy, one-story bungalow with big windows and wood floors. It smelled of ocean and long-ago pup, and it only took Gem a few minutes to sniff out a dog bed tucked under the sofa. Laughing and sighing at the same time, Laurel pulled it out, inviting Gem to try it. Gem sniffed the edges, circled, plopped down, and immediately sprang back up—this was no time for a nap. The bed was extra large and had a thick cushion. It would definitely do!

Laurel opened the back door to complete the tour, and they both walked out into the small rear yard. There was a little patch of grass and a couple of raised beds for vegetables and flowers. A fig and an apple tree were tucked into two corners. Everything was fresh and green and growing because winter in California was warm and moist.

There was a smell in the air that was new to Gem, too, a salty briny smell. And the wind seemed to breathe, in and out, never stopping completely.

"I've got one more load to bring in from the car," Laurel told her. "And then we can go to the beach!" Her trip to the Prius was quick, and after filling a big bowl with water for her new roommate, she threw on a pair of shorts and a long-sleeved T-shirt and grabbed a leash.

Out on the sidewalk, Gem knew which way to turn. She could smell *and* hear the destination! Plus, the setting sun was calling them to the beach. When they reached the long stretch of wide sand, they raced each other toward the water. Gem had never seen so much water before! It was bigger than the lake, and like the breezes it never stopped swirling in and out. It lapped at the shore, splashing and gurgling. Unable to resist, Gem threw herself into the foamy breakers, getting wet up to her stomach fur. She backed up as the wave retreated, sucking at her paws, then rushed back in. This big water liked to play!

"What do you think, Gem? You like the ocean?" Laurel said. Gem *loved* it! She lapped at the salty water, which cracked Laurel up. "It's not good for drinking, silly dog!"

Then Laurel showed Gem what the beach was really good for. She began to jog beside the waves.

Gem quickly matched her pace and they ran along the shore on the damp, hard-packed sand that the outgoing tide had left behind.

For the first time in a long time, Gem longed to race ahead, to run as fast as she could. Maybe it was the expanse of sand. Maybe it was the ocean. Maybe it was her arrival in her new forever home. Maybe it was Laurel. Whatever it was, her heart soared right out of her rosy chest, and she launched herself forward, taking several galloping strides. Panting, she stopped and turned back to wait for her new human and took the rest of the run at Laurel's pace. Her ears flopped while her paws pounded, and she inhaled surf and sand and seaweed.

The twosome jogged to the end of the beach and back, finishing up just as the sun descended on the horizon, igniting the sky in orange and yellow hues. Laurel tugged off her shoes, and they raced into the surf for a brief two-armed, six-legged swim in the cool, salty water. This time Gem went in until her feet no longer touched the bottom and paddled beside Laurel. When they emerged from the water together, they shook droplets from their hair and fur . . . Laurel had forgotten her towel again! Fortunately the air was warm even without the sun in the sky, and they found a thick drift-wood log several yards from the water where they could sit together and listen to the waves. They watched the sky continue to change from blue to orange to pink while Gem leaned into Laurel, tasting the salt on her whiskers and feeling the soft shifting sand under her paws.

As she felt the sand move, Gem's body twitched. She looked down. Sand! Under her paws! In an instant she was on her feet, digging into the forgiving earth and sending the tiny grains flying. When she got so deep she couldn't stand on the edge, she started another hole. Then another. And another. And the amazing thing? Gem wasn't searching or longing for anything while she dug—she had everything she needed. She was digging to dig. Digging for pleasure. Digging because she loved it!

Laurel watched, her eyes alight. She hadn't even realized that Gem would be in digging heaven here . . . her house was just a few blocks from the beach!

Satisfied with her work, Gem licked Laurel's damp arm, which was salty from the ocean. Both of them felt it. The sand, the sky, the ocean, themselves. They were all signs. They were meant to be here, together.

23

Gem loved everything about her new beach home. She loved the b-i-g bed that used to belong to another good dog. She loved waking up early with Laurel and running on the beach. She loved their other walks, their swims, and digging in the sand for the pure joy of it. She loved working alongside Laurel. Gem was an honorary Bark Ranger at Point Allende State Park, and when they worked Gem wore a special vest and Laurel wore a collared shirt, badge, and hat. On their days off Gem wore a different vest, for search and rescue training. The only thing Gem loved more than work was training days.

Every Saturday she and Laurel got up earlier than usual, went for a shorter run than usual, and drove south to meet up with three dog-human handler teams: Chip and Roger, Diva and Luke, and Opal and Meg.

When they first met, the four dogs circled and sniffed one another cautiously. Gem liked Diva instantly. She was a dainty Doberman with a prancy walk and a stub of a tail that was almost always moving. She and her handler, Luke, were already certified. Chip was a giant rottweiler-Labrador mix who smelled a little like fish. Like Gem, he was working to get SAR certified for urban search and rescue. Chip made the hairs at the base of Gem's tail tingle, but it didn't take long to realize that the massive rottweiler-Lab mix's big stance and deep bark were all bluster. He was actually very gentle and friendly . . . not to mention a search machine! Opal was a German shepherd mix who was also certified and had been deployed all over the country . . . her time in the field would be ending before too long. Still, she and her human handler, Meg, had a lot of knowledge to share with the newer recruits and never missed a training day.

Today, on their way to their session, Laurel pointed the Prius in a direction that wasn't familiar. Gem swallowed a whimper and lifted her nose to the crack in the window. They had turned inland, away from the ocean and away from the abandoned military base where they usually trained. As the smells of the things Gem adored got fainter and fainter, a whimper escaped her throat. She wanted to see her pack! She wanted to run drills! She wanted to track scents and find "victims"!

Gem pulled her head away from the window to look at Laurel, and a whiff of something *really* unusual hit her snout. It was reminiscent of the dark bonfire holes left on the beach, but with other scents mixed in—smells of charcoal and wood and grass.

As the odors got stronger, Laurel pulled off the road into a turnout. The area was black and nearly devoid of undergrowth, but the still-standing trees loomed straight and tall over it, their trunks and branches scorched and blackened.

"It's okay, Gem," Laurel assured the pup. "We're in a controlled burn area." She turned off the car and let Gem out.

Within minutes a couple of other cars pulled off the road, and Gem's tail wagged in relief. She recognized the SUV, the wagon, and the banged-up truck. The handlers all popped out of their vehicles—along with a couple of extra folks Gem didn't know—and soon the dogs were circling, sniffing, bowing, and tussling. Gem gave Diva a good long sniff, followed by a play bow and a soft bark. Opal received a friendly ear lick.

The blackened area looked desolate and smelled strange . . . being in it was unsettling, if also essential. They'd come here to train because fires were a regular hazard in California, and the dogs needed to learn how to discern the smells of people when they were immersed in the overwhelming acrid, smoky odors left by flames.

The two strangers—a round man who smelled like potato chips and a woman who smelled strongly of coffee and cream, walked off into the burn area. The dogs tussled a bit longer, then were called to their handlers.

"We're going to start with some simple finds," Luke said. The dogs were all used to (and skilled at) locating hiding victims. "It's the usual drill, but a bit harder in this environment." Since Luke was certified, he was the designated leader. He and Diva would watch all morning while the others trained.

Gem was eager to get to it. There were so many smells her nose was on overdrive . . . her paws were antsy. She didn't like the waiting! She needed to move, to search! Finally, Laurel strapped on Gem's red SAR vest, making her wag. When the vest was on she knew what was coming next! Laurel asked Gem to sit and there was a little *more* waiting while Chip and Opal got themselves situated with Roger and Meg. Then, after making eye contact with

Laurel, the word Gem was waiting for came in a chorus of voices. "Find!"

The dogs were off. Initially they clustered tightly together as they sniffed the ground. After a few minutes, they separated a bit, making ever-widening circles, choosing the scent path of one or the other victim and beginning to track. Gem followed her nose to an open area to the right of the pack and quickly moved along as she deciphered smells. She was tracking potato chips.

Gem found potato-chip man quickly, barking her alert as Chip approached. Laurel and Roger both arrived a few minutes later and awarded their dogs with liver treats and pets.

The next drill was similar, as was the one after that. The group ran drills all day and all over the burn area. Gem was successful, though in some areas it was harder to separate smells than in others. After a search in a particularly intense spot, the pups' paws started to feel hot and uncomfortable. The still-smoldering ground was scorching their footpads! All three handlers paused the search action to dig into their backpacks.

Gem stood still while Laurel strapped protective booties on each of her feet. It felt strange to have a barrier between her paws and the ground, and since they were new, they added another smell to the myriad already inundating her nose. She didn't like them!

"I know," Laurel said. "But you need them to protect your paws."

Gem had no idea what she was actually saying, though the meaning was clear. The booties were staying.

For the next couple of hours, Gem and Chip went neck and neck on their finds, taking turns being first to sniff out coffee and potato chips. Opal managed to find first a couple of times, too. Treats, pets, and games of tug were plentiful.

"Okay, let's take a break," Luke called after Gem bested Chip for the second time in a row. They gathered in an open space surrounded by blackened scrub pine. "Our guest victims have to head out, so for the rest of the session the four handlers will take turns hiding while the dogs search in a pack."

The dogs went a little berserk when they realized that their own handlers were hiding . . . especially Diva, who'd been watching the trainings all morning. She raced through the burn area like a mad dog, and kept up with Gem . . . who eked out the lead and found Luke half-buried behind a rare unburned fallen trunk. On the second round, Gem was first to reach Meg, easily outpacing the other dogs.

"I think she's peeking," Meg joked as she got to her feet. Her pants were covered in dark smears of ash—dogs and humans alike were all smeared and spotted, in fact.

Finally it was Laurel's turn to hide, and despite her attempt to make the find a challenge, Gem located her so fast the handlers agreed that Laurel should hold her back on the next round to give the other dogs a chance. She definitely had the skills needed for certification!

Laurel crouched down so she was eye to eye with Gem and threw her arms around the golden's neck. She couldn't imagine life without her new companion! Gem sensed the happiness and pride and love wafting off of Laurel, and it made *her* feel happy and proud, too. Her chest was light as she leaned in and licked Laurel's face all over. She was so content that she didn't mind staying right by her side while the other dogs kept "finding."

When they loaded up half an hour later, the whole group was happy and tired and filthy. To celebrate their success, Laurel and Gem stopped for a cleansing and celebratory dip in the ocean on their way home. And this time, Laurel had two towels at the ready . . . one for each of them!

24

One morning, when the days had started to get noticeably shorter, Gem awoke early, her nose twitching. She smelled smoke. It wasn't the campfire smoke she knew, or even the scorchy smell from the burn area where they'd recently trained. This was different. This smoke was filled with odors of more than burning wood . . . a lot more. It held the scents of burning plastic and metal, of concrete. It was a chemical smell that made her lungs ache.

Getting up off her bed, she walked over to a window and stared out. The sky was dark. Not night dark, but like someone had covered it with a thick gray blanket, blocking the sun. Gem whimpered and went to wait by the door, next to her leash and Laurel's running shoes.

"Not today, girl," Laurel said a little apologetically. "Fall is fire season, and the air is awful out there. It's not safe to breathe." She walked to the back door. The wrong door. "You'll have to do your business in the yard today . . ." Gem tilted her head, confused. She hardly ever went in the yard! Eventually, though, she understood. Her tail lower than usual, she took care of things on the small patch of grass between the raised beds.

The two spent the day at home, with Laurel reading and Gem trying to sit still but in fact spending more time pacing in front of the door. "It's a bad fire season," Laurel told her repeatedly. "And we can't go out when it's smoky." Gem had no idea what she was saying, but did know that she felt icky. She wanted her nose to stop itching. She wanted her lungs to stop aching. She wanted to run and dig at the beach!

The smoke lasted for weeks, with Gem getting used to, but hating, being stuck inside. When at last the air cleared a bit, she and Laurel went back to work at Point Allende, where they led tours and provided information about the local wildlife to visitors. Gem was thrilled to be out of the house but could tell that Laurel was worried about something. For one thing, she had that sour apprehensive smell, like apple cider vinegar. For another, her movements were stiffer and tighter than usual. She didn't talk to Gem as much as she usually did, either—she spoke more to herself in a low mumble. And there was a wrinkle between her eyebrows that never went away. On the weekend they trained, but only a little bit.

On Saturday a week later, Laurel climbed out of bed looking and smelling both worried and hopeful. She reached for her phone and checked her email first thing. The air quality had been improving steadily. Though the hills had been burning for weeks, the flames were contained and the winds had shifted at last, clearing out the ashy smog and bringing in cleaner air. Everyone could breathe easier again, both literally and figuratively. Laurel had been grateful all along that dogs weren't deployed during fires—their grueling job was to search for cadavers afterward—but was also grateful that the danger to everyone was now significantly reduced.

She tapped her screen and saw that the email she'd been waiting for had come in. A little breathless, she opened it and began to read . . .

"Oh my gosh!" she exclaimed, looking over at Gem. "The certification test is happening! It's on, Gem!"

The final test had been scheduled weeks ago, but with the local wildfires Laurel half assumed it would be postponed since emergency personnel had been tapped for weeks on end. But here it was, the notice that the test was a go. Excitement and concern blasted through her at the same time. The big Southern California blaze had limited their training, and now it was time for them to show their stuff.

They didn't have a lot of time to get ready, but Laurel knew Gem would need to run off as much energy as possible, so they headed out for a beach romp. After a hearty breakfast (that was harder for Laurel to get down than Gem), Laurel prepared her backpack. "I hope we remember everything!" she said, grabbing Gem's leash off its hook.

At the testing site, there were lots of dogs and handlers Gem had never seen or smelled before. But there were also a couple of dogs she'd met at the beach, and Chip and Roger! Everyone was in the same situation—being tested after training time had been severely limited. The air crackled with anticipation and excitement. Gem felt tingly, too. Her legs were twitchy. She wanted to run and run and run!

Laurel strapped the red SAR vest onto a visibly vibrating Gem. They were both thrumming with excess energy. To get a little out, they jogged the perimeter of the testing grounds a couple of times . . . then a couple more.

Gem ran proudly alongside her handler. Her vest felt snug. Her body felt strong. She was ready to smell. She was ready to find. She was r-e-a-d-y!

The team was going for urban/suburban SAR and FEMA certification. To pass, they'd need to show skills in two main areas, the first of which was trailing.

Laurel called Gem to her side and into a sit. "Good girl, Gem," she said, laying a steadying hand on the back of her neck. They both waited for the tester's "go" signal. When it came, Laurel asked Gem to find, and Gem put her nose to the ground and began her search.

The trail she was following had been left by a group of testers and was "aged," which meant that it had been left six hours before so that the scent had time to dissipate and would be harder to follow. Per protocol, the trail had also been contaminated by other smells—garbage, petroleum products, building materials, and other pungent stuff. The victim could be anywhere and buried under anything—as far as a mile away.

Laurel struggled to keep up with Gem as the golden retriever followed her quivering nose all over the vast site. Pausing to catch her breath, Laurel wondered if Gem was on the right path. They hadn't trained in weeks, and with so many scents and distractions . . . well, it was a little unnerving.

She told herself not to worry—Gem knew what she was doing. Gem was a natural. But as she saw the pup's tail disappear into a tangle of bushes she felt uncertain. She took a deep breath and followed.

A few minutes later, Gem barked out her alert, and Laurel was flooded with relief and a little touch of guilt. She never should have doubted her Gem!

Back near their starting point, the team was granted a short break before their second test, which would be harder. Laurel kept Gem next to her and on a lead while the tester explained. In front of them were several intentionally collapsed buildings used to train firefighters and other first responders. Laurel looked up at the huge, spooky-looking structures and felt a bit of trepidation. Gem, though, wagged with excitement!

"For this test we want you to let the pups range," the tester said. "Your dog should basically be working solo, with you hanging back."

Laurel nodded, signaling that she understood. She took a deep breath to clear her mind. She had to be steady and calm. Gem could handle this, and so could she.

"Begin!" the tester called. Gem walked around the edge of the massive, partially destroyed buildings before jumping up onto a porch with a cracked floor. Laurel held her breath as Gem's rosy-golden tail disappeared in the wreck. It was never easy for her to let Gem range, because it triggered her fear of losing her. She much preferred to keep her jewel of a dog close!

Inside, Gem scrambled over a teetering pile of

rubble, her tail swaying back and forth. It reminded her of the big pile at the Sterling ranch. Her feet were fleet and sure as she ducked under bent rebar and over concrete crumbles. She sniffed all over the building she was in and then crawled back out and moved on to the second, leaving no stone unsmelled.

As she approached the door of a third building, her nose detected the thing she was looking for . . . a live human! She zeroed in, moving quickly toward a doorway. The door itself was off its hinges and blocking the entry, so she scampered up a piece of lumber and through a window. The scent was not as strong here, so she backtracked down a short hallway, climbing over broken Sheetrock and pipes, and then back to the door that was off its hinges. Gem's whole body buzzed as she got closer to the victim she knew was there. A minute later, she found the spot! She couldn't see him but knew for certain he was beneath this pile of rubble.

"Woof!" Gem barked her alert. Here! She barked

until she heard people—and smelled Laurel—on the other side of the door. They moved the slab of wood aside and Laurel hurried over to find Gem pawing at the spot where the victim had buried himself. When the victim had been sprung and the test completed, they returned to their starting point to receive their official congratulations. Gem knew she had done well—she could tell by the way Laurel smelled and the expressions on all the human faces. She felt waggy all over! The humans shook hands, making it official. Gem was certified!

25

When they left the testing area, Laurel drove straight to the closest In-N-Out Burger and the pair celebrated with a Double-Double combo. Gem got one of the burger patties, a few fries, and a lot of petting. After the fast-food fest, life for the certified SAR team in the beach house went back to the way it had been before the local firestorm, which was fine with Gem. She and Laurel woke up early every morning. They ran on the beach, swam, and worked at Point Allende State Park. On the weekends they skipped the work, slept in a little, and spent extra time at the shore. They dug holes, watched sunsets, chased seagulls and waves, and curled up on the couch together when it got dark. The only things that interrupted their routine were the less frequent training days—to keep up certification—and the more frequent wildfires as California's dry season continued.

And then the fires stopped and the rains came.

At first the rains were welcome. They cleared the smoky air and made everything feel fresh and new. The storms didn't stop Laurel and Gem from running or swimming, either. In fact, Gem liked running in the rain as much as running in sunshine—maybe more. The drops kept the paths and dry sand from getting too hot under her feet and felt good on her lolling tongue.

But too much of a good thing could sometimes become a bad thing.

The rains continued for several weeks. Then a storm came and stayed. And stayed. And stayed. It rained steadily for days on end—the clouds refused to allow the sun through for even a moment.

Without the sunshine, Laurel began to wilt like a plant in a closet. Gem observed her person anxiously. She seemed to droop even more in the evenings, when they watched the news and listened to the water drip, drip, drip outside. In the morning she didn't always get up to run.

To cheer her up one evening, Gem climbed onto the couch and settled heavily on top of her.

"Ooof! Gemmy! You're too big to be a lapdog," Laurel had laughed. But only for a second. Her smile disappeared as Gem rearranged herself so that only her head rested on Laurel's leg. She pet Gem absently, her eyes glued to the glowing, talking screen several feet away.

Laurel had lived through droughts and fires in California before—they came with the territory, along with earthquakes. The current situation, though, was new to her. The bad fire season followed closely by such extreme, saturating rains was creating dangerous conditions. The bushes, trees, and grasses had all been burned away. The charred and barren hills were left exposed. Without living root systems to hold the earth in place, it was washing away in the endless rain. Not only was the heavy downpour stripping the fertile topsoil, it was seeping in and destabilizing the mountains.

Laurel gnawed on a thumbnail like a stressed-out dog working over a chew toy. "They're evacuating," she said aloud.

Gem lifted her head to look at Laurel's face, then resettled and pressed her chin down on the runner's muscular leg. All she could do to calm her person was to be here, to lean in and wag slowly.

After taking a deep breath and releasing it, Laurel closed her eyes for a long moment. All fall she'd prayed for rain to help contain fires. Now she prayed for it to stop before the mountains came crashing down on the houses below.

Luckily the danger zone did not include their neighborhood, which was flat enough and far enough away from the hills to be safe. Her heart went out to the people being asked to evacuate.

Many of them had animals that had to be moved safely and quickly. She couldn't imagine the stress! She watched news footage of folks coaxing their horses into trailers to drive them far from the unsound hills, and more footage of people refusing to leave. As a trained rescue worker, she knew the importance of being prepared, listening to the warnings, and doing what the authorities advised for your own safety and the safety of others. She kept a backpack of essentials in her car and a second one in a little closet by the door. She worried for everyone who had to grab and go—prepared or not. And she especially worried for the people who were not heeding the warning . . . the people who'd decided to stay in spite of it.

That night in bed, Gem lay curled up on her thick cushion on the floor. She listened to Laurel, waiting for her breathing to become soft and regular, the way humans breathed when they were asleep. But Laurel's breathing didn't change. It sounded as though she was fighting with her covers. Punching her pillow. Rolling over and over. At last Laurel's breath grew steady and even. Gem closed her own eyes and was snoring softly within seconds.

Sometime in the night Gem woke up. It was dark. The rain had slowed. She heard a distant rumble—or maybe she felt it—or both. It was far away and reminded her of the sound of crashing waves. But it was not the ocean. It was farther away and in the wrong direction. Gem whimpered, and Laurel's hand dropped over the edge of the bed onto her head. "It's okay," Laurel mumbled sleepily. But the hair on Gem's neck and back still stood at attention. It was not okay, and Gem knew it.

26

The call came early, even before Gem had gotten them up to pee. The anxious dog had barely slept after the strange rumble in the night. She could feel that something was amiss, and it felt like something big.

Laurel must have sensed something was off, too. She answered her phone on the first ring and without an ounce of sleepiness in her voice. Though she'd been dreaming a moment before, she felt wide-awake as she said, "Hello."

Sitting up, she held the phone to her ear. She looked right at Gem as she listened. "Uh-huh.

Uh-huh . . . No. We've never been deployed as a team before . . . No, we haven't trained for this scenario exactly . . . Yes, we're up for it. Of course. Of course. I'm sure. Text me the address."

Gem never looked away, and Laurel felt like her dog might be reading her mind. "This is it, Gemmy," she told the pup. "They need us. Now."

Laurel started pulling on clothes before she even made it to the bathroom. She opened the back door for Gem to go out, but Gem just looked at her. The pup could feel the tension. She didn't want to miss a second.

"Okay." Laurel shrugged. It was good that dogs didn't have to wait to have working plumbing every time they wanted to relieve themselves. "This could be a long day," she said. "Or week," she added, mostly to herself.

Laurel poured two bowls of breakfast, one granola and one kibble. She ate her cereal with yogurt, standing next to Gem. It didn't feel right to sit down, and adrenaline was already coursing through her body. They needed to get to the address she'd been given over the phone as quickly as possible. Time was of the essence. Honestly, it didn't feel right to eat, either, but she forced the food down. Her body would need the fuel.

Gem crunched her last dry food nugget and glanced up at the still-eating Laurel. She paced. She held back an anxious whine. Finally, Laurel put her bowl in the sink and got out Gem's vest. The good dog sat still while Laurel fastened and adjusted her SAR wear.

"Ready, girl?" Laurel asked. She knelt in front of her dog and looked into her eyes. Gem wasn't able to decipher all of Laurel's words, but she understood their meaning. Laurel was certain of that. "There was a massive mudslide last night. People are trapped. We need to go and find them before their time runs out."

Gem felt the urgency in Laurel's voice and heard the concern, too. When the front door opened, she was the first to the car.

The slide wasn't far away, but it felt like it took forever to get there. Laurel tuned in to the local news on the radio to see if she could get more information. She kept her eyes on the road as she listened to the special disaster coverage. It sounded bad. Her fingers gripped the steering wheel tighter and tighter until her knuckles were white, and she had to remind herself to take a deep breath and loosen her grip.

The worst of the landslide predictions—the ones that had been making it hard for her to sleep at night—had come true. In the early dawn the rains filled the creeks beyond capacity. The waters overflowing the banks added to the heavy satura-tion levels, and the hillsides above the community of Madrona began to slough and slide. Thick riv-ers of mud coursed down roadways, gathering speed and debris. The mudflows surged through the neighborhoods, overwhelming everything in their paths—cars, trees, entire houses—gathering more and more wreckage as they careened through. When they finally slowed and stopped, there was nothing but ruin in their wakes.

According to the reporters getting a bird's-eye view from helicopters, the debris field—the area buried in mud and slurry and wreckage—covered more than eighteen square miles.

Laurel pulled into the parking lot of the local high school that they would be using as their base of operations. A few stray raindrops splattered against the windshield. She turned off the engine and put her hand on Gem's neck. "Ready?" she asked. Gem gave her cheek a lick. "Me too," she said. "As ready as I'll ever be, anyway." Though she'd been a search and rescue worker for over a decade and had seen a lot of disasters, she was having trouble picturing what they were about to see and experience.

Their team was mostly assembled and already getting briefed when Laurel and Gem walked up. It was good to see familiar faces and tails. Meg, Opal, Roger, and Chip were there. Laurel also recognized a few other local fire SAR teams being loaded into the back of a large army vehicle designed to travel in high water. They exchanged hellos, tight smiles, and mellow tail wags. This wasn't exactly a happy reunion.

Laurel stood beside the wheel of the high-water truck, waiting to get in. The tire came up to the top of her shoulder. She lifted Gem up to Roger, who grabbed the strap on her vest to hoist her into the big tarp-covered truck bed, then climbed in herself and took a seat beside Roger on the benches that lined the sides. Dogs and equipment sat on the floor in the center.

When everyone was loaded, they rolled out. The truck turned onto a road, but quickly the vehicle left the smooth pavement and began to bump and lurch along. Out of the opening in the back Laurel saw only thick mud and ruin—the roads were indiscernible. They traveled slowly, making their way closer to the epicenter of the flash flooding and mudslides. The dogs panted near their handlers' feet. The rescue workers leaned in to try to see as much as they could. It was all a shock.

Laurel closed her eyes for a second, realizing that *nothing* could have prepared her for this. The world outside looked like an alien landscape. There were rock fields with boulders the size of cars smashed against the remains of houses. Power lines were not only down, they were twisted around trees and structures and sometimes completely invisible in the mud. Entire cars, even large SUVs, were buried in muck. She saw other cars with their wheels gone, stripped off by the force and speed of the debris wave as it streamed past.

Beside her, Roger took in a sharp breath as he spotted what used to be a home and was now just a sludge-covered foundation. There were large pieces of roof on the ground around it and more hanging in broken trees.

The truck bounced and finally jerked to a stop to allow the SAR crew to climb slowly down. Outside the sheltered bed of the emergency vehicle, the devastation was even more overwhelming. It went on in all directions, and when Laurel looked closer, she saw toys and bicycles and dishes and toothbrushes—regular objects of all shapes and sizes—littered throughout . . . relics from normal life just a day before.

Gem jumped down and stood next to Laurel. Her handler's anxiousness was palpable, so she stepped closer and leaned against Laurel's legs to let her know she was there. They were together. And Gem was ready to get to work.

Laurel put her hand on the top of Gem's head and nodded in response to the unanswered question. She was ready, too, because they both knew that out there, in all that mess, there were people. People hidden and trapped and struggling to hold on. People hoping to be found. People waiting to be rescued.

27

The unloaded teams huddled around Alana Eggleton, the county task force leader. More teams, at least a dozen of them, were coming from all over California and a few neighboring states, but the local teams were the first on the scene. Alana was wearing a hard hat and safety vest and carrying a large pole. She cautioned the workers to take their safety very seriously—with the downed power lines and inability to see what was under the surface of the mud, the level of risk was extremely high. Laurel settled her own hard hat on her head.

"The moving mud and debris is dangerous and

powerful. It also leaves pockets and voids. These spaces are precisely what we need to find and search, because they are the places where people can survive," Alana explained. "We think the area we're in now has the highest potential for survivors. We need to search homes and cars." She instructed everyone to look for cars still in or near driveways and garages. Many people had been sleeping when the slide hit, and unfortunately this neighborhood had not been evacuated. The searchers passed around poles for probing the thick mud, and cans of bright orange paint so they could mark areas that had been searched. Laurel slipped the can into one of her vest pockets, anxious to begin. There was a lot of ground to cover.

Alana dispatched small groups to specific areas and explained that there were some places that they wouldn't be able to reach by land because the roads were impassable, even with the military vehicles. In those cases teams would need to be flown in to search via helicopters, because excavating the streets would take too much time—time they didn't have.

Laurel peered down the mud-covered road they were standing on. In the near distance, past a huge snarl of tree limbs, she saw a boulder the size of a shed blocking an entire lane. She exhaled slowly. This wasn't even the hardest-hit spot!

"Okay." Alana held up her radio. "Be safe. Be in touch. Stick together."

The teams moved out. Laurel looked at Roger and then Chip, who had been assigned to a team with her and Gem. They'd have to have one another's backs. Using their poles to probe the muddy depths and feel for anything unusual, Roger and Laurel slogged toward the nearest structures . . . or what was left of them. Gem and Chip hopped up onto the objects protruding from the muck, balancing on tree limbs, bits of wall, car roofs . . . anything that was above the muck. Their noses were on overdrive, perpetually scanning for human scent.

Gem smelled scores of people, which was normal for her. She was used to training with lots of humans around. This devastated area was populated with all kinds of emergency responders in addition to search teams. Local residents were out searching, too.

It was easy for Laurel to tell the difference between rescue workers and the people who lived in the area. Besides their hard hats, radios, and tools, the professional responders looked grim and determined. The residents, in contrast, wore everyday clothes. Many were still in pajamas. They had haunted looks in their eyes, and moved like zombies in horror films. Gem jumped onto a low stone wall that was still standing, and wagged closer to a mud-covered man who had stopped to lean against a truck with muck up to its floorboards.

The man reached out to absently pet Gem, leaving a streak of brown on her reddish-golden head. He spoke to everyone and no one at once.

"It was so *loud*," he said, shaking his head.

"I heard it coming. It woke me up. It sounded like a thousand freight trains . . . like the end of the world. And when it hit the house it just . . . I just . . . I looked back and they were gone. They were all gone." He covered his mouth with a mud-caked hand and stared, glassy-eyed, into the distance.

Laurel wasn't sure what to do or say. She wanted to ask who "they" were, but understood it was his family.

Gem pushed her head into the man's leg so he could feel her warmth. She didn't want him to feel lost. She wanted him to know that she was there.

"We're here to find everyone we can," Laurel finally said. "We're here to help."

Gem barked her agreement, and the man tucked his chin once, still staring.

Chip and Roger had kept moving toward the structures, and Laurel peered after them, anxious to catch up and stick together. She tucked Gem's lead into her vest and looked to her dog. "Find," she told Gem. The command worked for both specific and nonspecific scenting of humans. Gem was practiced at locating hidden people—she knew the targets were not the humans she could spot easily using just her eyes.

Gem followed in the direction that Chip had gone. The mud slurped at her feet, pulling them down. It wasn't smooth mud, either. There were sharp rocks and sticks and lots of other things in it that scraped her legs and paws. *Squlech. Slurp. Schlop.* She continued as best she could toward the nearest collapsed home.

The garage door of the house had been pummeled. It hung askew and was blocked by a fallen tree, a tangle of branches, an upended basketball hoop, and a surfboard. Laurel's heart jumped into her throat as Gem expertly climbed into what looked like a surfing pterodactyl's nest. The agile pup hopped onto the wider trunk of the tree and off again, sliding into a narrow space to enter the garage.

The entire house had been forced off its

foundation and was tilted at a crazy angle. The west corner was completely buried in mud. Laurel blinked at it, watching the spot where Gem had disappeared.

The tossed-and-turned nature of the mudslide destruction was disturbing. It was the kind of damage Laurel would have expected to see after a hurricane or a tornado. Then she remembered footage she'd seen of a beachside town after a tsunami had hit—water with debris mixed into it was as chaotic and deadly as swirling, gale-force winds. Maybe even more so.

Without taking her eyes off the dark sliver of space where Gem had entered the slanting mess, Laurel scrambled onto a car-sized boulder sitting in the middle of what used to be a wide driveway. A low retaining wall bordering the driveway was still partly visible. She strained to see any movement or catch a tiny glimpse of golden fur.

Inside the collapsed garage, Gem moved cautiously. The smells were jumbled, and she huffed air in and out to try to capture and identify the scents. Smells almost always seemed sharper in the dark, and she easily detected a mix of sewage and natural gas coming from broken pipes. She picked up the earthier smells of splintered wood and wet soil. Jumbled-up smells from wet fabrics, smashed foodstuffs, drywall. She froze and inhaled. Exhaled. Inhaled. She did not smell any victims.

By crouching and crawling commando-style, Gem was able to wriggle back out of the space. She looked for Laurel as soon as she emerged.

Laurel saw a fuzzy head appear and had to keep from cheering. She climbed carefully off of her boulder perch to mark the spot as "searched" while Gem moved on to her next task.

Behind the garage, a tangle of cyclone fencing that wrapped around a half-toppled tree was easy to scale. Gem climbed up to see and sniff what lay beyond. It looked like a flattened yard area . . . fairly free of debris. She hopped down to explore further, but the second her paws touched the brown muck below, Gem knew she'd made a mistake. The ground was not solid. It wasn't even just soft! In an instant she was swallowed up by thick muck that closed quickly over her head. She pumped her legs, but there was nothing solid beneath them to help her. The dense liquid that surrounded her was thicker than water and thinner than mud. It filled her nose and mouth. She struggled to lift her head. She couldn't see. She couldn't breathe. She could barely hear. The shrill scream of Laurel's emergency whistle penetrated her dark, liquefied prison. A moment later there was nothing.

28

A strong hand grabbed Gem by the scruff and yanked her up and out of the deadly slurry. Coated in a thick layer of sludge, she landed on Laurel's lap. Laurel threw her arms around her dog's chest and squeezed hard to push water out and let air into her lungs.

Gem coughed up muck. She coughed and coughed while Laurel held her tight, now squeezing her out of relief and love. "Oh, Gem! My Gem. Oh. I thought I'd lost you!" It was one of the quickest and scariest things Laurel had ever seen. She'd caught sight of Gem as she reached the top of the fencing and then watched as Gem jumped down and just . . . disappeared. It was like the earth swallowed her whole! She watched her dog sink into the deep mud in the blink of an eye. Using her pole, she'd miraculously found a solid place to climb down and plunged her arm into the spot where her dog had gone under. Thank goodness Gem hadn't sunk down too deep. Thank goodness Laurel had been able to reach her and haul her back up.

"Get it out," Laurel said, happy to hear Gem's coughing, even as she worried about what she might have swallowed.

"Is everyone okay?" Roger yelled down from his perch on the rubble above them. He'd come as soon as he heard Laurel's whistle. He squinted at the dark brown, four-legged mass getting to its feet beside Laurel. The shape shook and muck flew everywhere. "Is that Gem?" Roger asked. Laurel nodded and held up her hand for Roger and Chip to stay where they were. She grabbed Gem's vest, too. She wasn't about to let her slip under again!

"Keep back," she wheezed. "I think we're right at the edge of a swimming pool! It's filled with mud."

Roger's eyes went wide. "Holy moly!" he exclaimed. The surface of the pool looked like solid ground but was in fact deadlier than quicksand. "Stay, Chip," he called to his dog. He gave a hand signal to the pup and reached down to help Laurel and Gem clamber to safety, or at least onto slightly more solid ground. He shuddered. The hazards left in the wake of the slide were countless and unknown. Even though they were skilled and trained, they all needed to proceed with extra caution.

Gem shook again and sent a few more globs of mud flying. She sneezed mud out of her nose and Laurel poured water from her bottle onto her dog's face and eyes. After all that her face was a pale brown, and the rest of her remained covered in thick, stinky mud. Not a single inch of her golden coat could be seen.

Gem was so happy to be free of the smothering muck that she licked Laurel's hand and wagged, splattering anything that wasn't already coated. Her nose twitched, and when she bowed her head to lick one of her paws, Laurel stopped her.

"I don't need you getting any more of this gunk inside of you!" she said. Laurel's nose wrinkled. "It smells. Who knows what's mixed up in here?"

Gem licked her lips. The mud tasted worse than it smelled.

Chip sniffed his canine friend. His legs looked mud-dipped, and his coat was a patchwork of crusty brown spots. He let out a soft whimper.

Roger and Laurel exchanged a look. "I just . . . I . . ." Laurel was not sure what to do next. She looked around at what had once been someone's backyard, pool house, and garden . . . She tried to wrap her head around the combination of rocks, trees, cars, and portions of walls mixed together with the tiny signs of yesterday's life that half-protruded from the mud . . . a Barbie, a shoe, a framed family picture, a teaspoon. Twenty-four hours ago things here had been normal, or at least intact. Tears filled her eyes. She felt overwhelmed—like Gem in the pool. The feeling threatened to consume her, but she managed to blink back the panic. It *couldn't* be too much. It *was* real. She *was* here. They were all here, to help. They were needed. She took a deep breath and stroked her dog's coated neck.

Steeling herself, Laurel got to her feet. She and Gem needed to do what they knew how to do . . . search for humans. Gem, though nearly unrecognizable, was ready to get back to work, too. Almost . . .

"Laurel, your diamond dog is looking pretty rough. I think you need to hose her down and make sure she's okay under that scuba suit of goop before we can get back to work," Roger advised. He pointed them toward the truck, which was equipped with a large barrel of water and a hose.

"Of course." Laurel nodded. Gem's safety—and her own—had to come first.

After a thorough dousing, the brown-black mud ran off of Gem in rivulets and her ruddy hue reemerged like the rising sun.

"There she is," Laurel said, applying a gentle cleanser she carried in her pack to make sure no toxins remained. Gem would have to have another bath at the end of each search day—they all would—but this was good enough for now. When she was done with the washing, Laurel checked Gem all over for cuts or swelling. She inspected her paws and between her toes and looked into her eyes. All clear.

Gem accepted the bath and lapped up a cool drink of clean water. Then she looked at Laurel expectantly. All in all she was feeling pretty good!

Alana came to check on the team. "Roger told me what happened. You two can call it a day and get some rest," she offered. Her eyebrows were arched in concern.

"Oh, no. Please." Laurel spoke for both of them. "We want to stay." The last thing she and Gem wanted was to be done for the day. They wanted to get back out there and do what they'd come to do. They wanted to help. "Right, Gem?" Laurel looked at the wet dog beside her. Gem's eyes glittered. Then, with a bark, she confirmed that neither of them was ready to call it quits.

Alana almost laughed. Instead she smiled with admiration and nodded. "Okay," she said. "Go get 'em."

29

Gem moved through a muddy, rock-and-branch-strewn area toward a half-crushed building that was once a detached garage. She knew now how the ground could look solid but not be—especially *behind* houses. The places where cars were parked were safer for walking and climbing, so she tried to stay in those areas. She did not want to get sucked into anything like that awful mud pit again. It was too scary.

Her nose quivered as she made her way through the twisted obstacle course. She smelled so many things that weren't usually mixed together, and it took a lot of concentration to decipher them all. Plus, she still had to pay attention to where she was walking! The mud slurped at her paws with each step, and she had to pull them back up—sometimes hard. When she finally reached the partially smashed garage, she turned back to make eye contact with her handler.

Laurel was following, but with only two legs and more body weight, she sank deeper into the glop. Her progress was slow. At that moment she was navigating a fallen tree trunk that blocked her path, so it took a few seconds for her to look up. She quickly assessed, then nodded at Gem. Gem held still another moment for a deep, nose-clearing sniff, and then crawled up onto a pile of tree roots and debris. She scrambled forward until she found a plank of wood that made an impromptu bridge across a muddy chasm to a broken window. She made her way across without any trouble and stuck her snout through the broken glass. What did she smell? This was harder than any training she had ever done! She stuck her nose in a little farther and smelled again. Was anybody in there? She wasn't sure. She had to go in.

Crouched on the fallen tree trunk, Laurel watched Gem's progress. She saw the back of her dog's head surrounded by large, triangular shards of glass sticking out from the window frame. She felt an urge to call Gem off. An injured dog would be of no use to the search team! But before she could open her mouth, Gem had already leaped through the window and disappeared.

Laurel inhaled sharply and hopped down off the tree trunk, then paused to listen for any sounds of alarm. A whimper. A yelp. She didn't hear anything. When she reached the heap of tree roots and debris Gem had scrambled up, she carefully climbed up herself. At the top she saw it was too dangerous for her to cross the makeshift bridge. She couldn't follow her dog. With a tense sigh, she sat down to wait.

30

The moment her body was through the window, Gem realized how far away the ground was on the other side—too far. She had no choice but to free-fall to whatever lay below, and somehow managed to land on the roof of a car that stuck out from the several feet of mud that had flowed in to cover the garage floor. Her paws clicked and then slid on the curved metal roof, sending her into a kind of four-legged split. She scrambled for a moment and then forced her strong leg muscles to pull her paws in toward one another until she was upright.

She paused to get her bearings. Standing on the

roof of the car, Gem lifted her head high and sniffed. She detected lots of things . . . metal and gasoline and the myriad odors wafting from the liquefied earth . . . but no humans. The more time she had on the scene, the more skilled her nose became at sorting out the unique smells created in the slide, which made it easier to single out the one thing she was looking for: living victims.

There was no need to stay in here. She lifted her nose, searching for a draft or a whiff of fresh air that might lead her to an easier exit . . . one that wouldn't require her to leap through the shards of glass she had managed to avoid on her way in.

She detected nothing. There was no other way out.

She whimpered quietly as she stood there, her claws slowly sliding away from one another on the metal roof of the car. She wished she could see Laurel. Just a glimpse of her person would give her strength. Instead she gazed up at the window she'd just come through. It was several feet above her.

There was a low roof rafter she could jump to, but, like the rest of the roof structure, it was broken. It could be wobbly.

"Gem?" Laurel's voice drifted through the window. She wasn't right there, but she *was* out there, somewhere. Not too far away. Waiting. "Gem?" Laurel called again, louder and firmer this time.

The sound of Laurel's voice helped Gem get moving. She leaped onto the rafter and braced as loosely as she could for balance. She heard the wood creak under her weight and felt it drop several inches before catching on another beam below. Gem waited until everything was still again. She eyed the window. There was definitely enough space for her to get through—she'd made it *in*— but coming at it from below would be harder . . . a lot harder.

Outside, Laurel was starting to panic. She could see the broken window with its shards of glass like teeth in a large, angry mouth, and nothing else. It made her think of circus lions jumping through

rings of fire. It didn't seem possible that any crea-
ture could come through unscathed. Laurel wished
she hadn't removed Gem's vest. It had been so
heavy with mud she was worried it would make
movement more difficult, or get caught on all the
wreckage, or . . . The worries were endless.

Inside the collapsing structure Gem lifted one
front paw, then put it down and lifted the other.
Her foot pads practically vibrated on the beam
beneath them—nerves and anticipation. She had
to leap, and leap perfectly. She steadied herself.
She crouched ever so slightly so as not to lose her
balance. Then, in a single, powerful motion, she
launched herself toward the window with every
ounce of strength she had, willing herself to fly
right through . . .

31

Gem sailed through the air toward the window, her front paws pointed directly at the middle of the opening. Her aim was solid, and her front legs soared through easily. She felt a little scrape on her left side as her torso cleared the frame. She was basically out! And then, just as her front paws touched the makeshift bridge, her back right leg snagged on the jagged edge of the window and twisted. A second later she landed with a whimper, steadying herself with three legs on the plank of wood.

Laurel winced as she watched her dog land and

tried to assess the situation from a distance. There was no way she could cross the bridge to where Gem was standing. They locked eyes for a long moment.

"Come, Gem," Laurel called gently.

Gem gingerly put weight on her hurt leg and made her way across much more slowly than she'd gone in the other direction. Laurel could see that she was limping, and felt an instant flash of dread. The hair on the back of her neck rose, and her breath sharpened. It reminded her how vulnerable dogs could be. Fear flooded in: Bluto's hidden heart problem, Gem's Lyme disease, which could reflare at any moment. Her eyes started to well with tears.

"Stop," Laurel told herself quietly so Gem wouldn't hear. "You saw her leg get caught. It was an accident; it's not an illness." She took a deep breath, and then another.

Gem was getting closer, and a few moments later Laurel was able to put her arms around her dog.

Her good dog Gem. She leaned her forehead into Gem's neck, ignoring the fresh mud, taking a moment. "Good girl, Gem," she told her. "Such a good girl." Just having the pup close helped Laurel gather strength. She got up on her knees, pushed her fear aside, and began a physical evaluation.

It wasn't easy to do an assessment on a dog who was half-coated in mud while sitting on a tangle of upended tree roots and debris, and Laurel briefly wondered if she should move to another area, or hose her down again, or get help from another rescue worker. She looked around and quickly realized that there was no better place nearby. She'd already used their fair share of precious water, and all the rescue workers were busy and overwhelmed. Besides, she reasoned, she knew Gem better than anyone.

Laurel took her time feeling everything and looking for injuries. Gem was patient with the process, even though it took several minutes. Miraculously, Gem didn't appear to be bleeding or even cut. But she did wince when Laurel pressed on her back right leg, down low.

"Sorry," Laurel told her. "I don't think either of us thought this deployment would turn into constant medical checks!" She gently felt all around Gem's hock joint, the spot above the paw that bends back, checking for mobility. It was definitely tweaked, and possibly sprained. She took off her backpack and rummaged around for a roll of medical tape. Wiping away some of the mud, she wrapped the joint as best she could. It wasn't her finest work, but would offer the leg a bit of support. As she finished, Gem leaned forward and licked Laurel's face, as if to tell her that everything was okay.

Laurel offered Gem a little bowl of water, which she happily lapped up, along with a bit of kibble. When the bowl was emptied, Gem thumped her tail on a broken tree root. Her leg was sore but not much. She wanted to work!

"Are you sure, girl?" Laurel asked. As prepared

as she was to keep going, she couldn't help but wonder if it was the right decision. She closed her backpack slowly, thinking. How far *could* they push their luck?

Gem was back on her paws—all four of them— and had her nose in the air. She thought maybe she'd just caught a faint whiff of human . . . live human! She let out an eager bark.

Laurel got to her own feet, nodding. "All right," she agreed. "Let's keep looking. People need us." She was smiling at her brave, wonderful dog as she gave the command to "find!"

32

Gem leaped down off the mass of tree roots, landing gently on all four legs. She put a fair amount of pressure on her sore leg to test it. She felt a twinge, but the pain wasn't bad. The wrapping Laurel had put on definitely helped! She picked her way around a mass of power poles and lines, and then a couple of boulders and another uprooted, broken tree. She was in mud up to her belly, but it was starting to feel normal.

The next house over was a smaller, single-story bungalow. Much of the back of it had been built with glass doors and windows, almost all of which had been smashed during the slide. The other exterior walls of the house were mostly buried in mud, and a section of the roof had been torn away. Gem could see a hole where the roof had been, about ten feet above where she stood. There it was again—the smell of human! It was stronger over here—she was on the right path.

She turned to Laurel, who was thigh-deep in muck at the moment and trying to navigate some utility poles. "It's okay, Gem," she called. "Find!"

Gem scrambled up a fallen, splintered tree trunk until she could see across to the opening in the roof. She panted a little as she looked inside, to give her nose a bit of a break. She'd have to jump . . . again. She looked back at Laurel . . . again. She saw her person nod the okay.

Gem stopped panting and took a deep whiff, capturing the scent cloud in the opening behind her nose. It was definitely there . . . human. Living, breathing human. She alternated the weight in her paws from one side to the other . . . back and forth on the tree trunk without moving forward. Back, forth. Back, forth. She stopped padding and crouched low. Finally, she leaped.

All this wild jumping was new to Gem. She'd had to take some leaps during training but never with such uncertainty. Gem didn't mind flying through the air—she kind of liked it—until it was almost time to land. About-to-land was the part she hated. She was glad it didn't last long.

This landing was much better than the others. It was all mud. It didn't taste very good and it splattered everywhere, but it didn't swallow her up or hurt her.

Laurel watched her dog disappear with another dive into something *else* she couldn't see, and swallowed hard. If she weren't knee-deep in sludge she would have paced. As it was, she could only get as close as possible and wait. She reminded herself that it was Gem's job to search, and her job to be there for Gem. She was doing the thing she'd been trained to do. They both were. "Trust," she told herself. "You have to trust."

Gem shook off as much mud as she could. She could feel a glob of it over her eye but could still see okay. She sneezed to get it out of her nose— smelling was essential! A giant boulder stood in the middle of the room with pieces of smashed furniture littered around it. Gem sniffed her way around the huge stone. The smell of human was stronger in here for sure. She stopped moving and pricked her ears to listen, but the sounds of rescue workers and machinery echoed throughout the neighborhood and filled her ears.

She sneezed out a little more mud. She had to focus on what she did best—sniffing. She ignored the smells of wood and metal and Sheetrock and concrete and mud, zeroing in on *human*. Human!

She moved slowly, letting the scent lead her. The smell was strongest in the hallway, but the entry to the passage was completely blocked by broken furniture and splintered wood. Gem let out a frustrated whimper and pawed at the bottom of the blockage. It gave way! She pawed again, and again . . . and moved the mud aside.

She kept at it, her paws digging and digging, creating a slippery path under a broken table and an upturned easy chair. Faster and faster she dug, to keep ahead of the mud that wanted to slide back into place. She stuck her nose through the blockade, and then her chest. Paw over paw over paw. And then, with a push, she was on the other side.

Gem got back up on all fours and shook. She'd made it through! This was the best she'd felt all day. Her mud-covered snout quivered. The smell of human was almost overwhelming!

33

Outside, Laurel watched a rescue worker "pole" the mud around the structures, sticking his long metal rod into the endless lake of brown gunk to feel for anything unusual beneath. She wished she could pole right now, too—that she had another job to do. One that kept her busy. Following Gem as she searched was making her feel a little useless, and helpless, even though it *was* her job. Between their scenting and physical abilities, dogs were far better equipped to do a higher level of searching and exploring. And they needed a human partner. Gem needed her.

Laurel took a sip of water and let out a slow breath. Knowing this and feeling okay about it were two different things. She preferred keeping busy at all times . . . she was a Doer with a capital D. Gem had been out of sight and in the house for twenty minutes now, and Laurel was getting twitchy. It was so hard to wait!

"She still inside?" one of the workers called from nearby.

Laurel turned to the voice and nodded. "Yes."

"That's probably a good sign," the worker said, pausing to wipe the mud from his face . . . and only succeeding in adding another smear. Everything and everyone was covered in muck. "Maybe she's found something."

Laurel felt her heart lift a bit. That was what she wanted to hope, too. Gem was skilled. If there were living people around, she would find them. She would! She took another sip of water, letting herself savor the cool, clean taste of it before swallowing. She sat back and waited for Gem's bark.

Inside the house, Gem squelched her way down the hallway. The door to a small closet had been ripped off its hinges, and bottles and jugs of cleaning supplies were scattered everywhere. A leaking bottle of bleach made Gem's nose tremble and almost blocked out the scent she was tracking. She kept going, one mud-slurping paw in front of another, letting her nose decipher the smells. Soon the chemical smell began to fade and the human scent came back into focus. She was getting closer!

A bark tried to escape her throat, but she held it in. She had to be certain there was a living person in here before alerting Laurel. She came across a giant heap of partially folded sheets and towels that had tumbled into the sludge and climbed over it.

The door to the bathroom was wide open, and also blocked by a large painting that had been knocked off the opposite wall. Gem lifted her nose, and there it was, even stronger . . . human.

Gem pawed at the bottom of the framed art, but

it didn't give. She couldn't dig it out of the way. Could she jump over it? She wasn't sure—the mud in the hall was holding her down. She whimpered a little and pawed higher. The canvas tore! She pawed at it some more and shoved in a paw. She ripped at the stiff fabric until there was a hole she could wriggle through.

Her nose detected everything as she moved past the frame, wiggling her hindquarters until they were free. She bounded forward, toward the claw-foot tub that was tipped on its side, and found what she was looking for. Curled inside was a teenage girl in the fetal position. Gem nosed her as gently as she could, then a teensy bit harder. She got no response. She leaned in close and gave her cheek a single lick. Warm breath swirled near her face! The girl was alive! Excited, Gem sat down and let out a bark. She barked and barked and barked!

34

The rescue worker, whose name was Erik, was still poling nearby when the faint sound of a bark reached Laurel's ears. Her head swiveled. That was a bark she'd know anywhere!

Erik saw Laurel's reaction. "We need quiet!" he called, holding his hands in the air. Arms straight up was a signal used to silence a disaster scene so that rescuers could hear a canine—or any other—alert signal. One by one, pairs of hands rose upward, and voices and machinery were silenced. Laurel's heart leaped into her throat. The muffled bark was easier to hear now. It was most definitely Gem, and it confirmed that she had found someone alive! Deep inside the wreckage, but alive!

Gem paused in her barking to scoot closer to the girl. The curled-up young teen didn't have as much heat coming off her body as most humans did. She felt cold, and Gem knew that wasn't good.

Gem licked the girl's hand and nosed her arm. She still wasn't moving, but Gem could feel shallow breath on her snout whenever she put it close to the girl's face. She lowered her body, curling in tight beside the motionless girl, trying to offer warmth. Once she was settled in close, she went back to barking.

Outside, a crew was preparing to deploy into the house—Erik, a second medic named Tommy, and Laurel were coming in. A crane operator maneuvered closer with his cherry picker, and they all squeezed onto the gated work platform attached to a hefty, motorized arm. A minute later the platform was being lifted high into the air, then rumbling closer to the house and the hole in the roof.

"Whoa," Laurel said as the heavy machine operator pulled levers and they descended into the living room. "That boulder is huge."

The platform came to a jolting halt just above the top of the mud and was locked in place. The team stepped off their mobile platform, the lower part of their legs quickly enveloped in mud. Laurel, who was keeping one ear on Gem's barks at all times, could tell that she was at the end of a hallway. The light was dim, but she could see that the passage was blocked. Knowing her dog and guessing how she would have tried to get through, Laurel looked down and spotted the trace of the tunnel Gem had created, already mostly refilled with muck.

"She dug her way through," Laurel told the other workers, dropping down to her knees and moving mud and debris aside with her hands.

"Smart dog," Eric said. "Tommy, let's try to clear some of this stuff while Laurel digs," he suggested.

Tommy nodded, and they moved a side chair, some kind of sculpture, and part of a bookshelf out of the way. Between the three of them, they were able to widen the passageway enough for humans to get through.

"Looks like the entire laundry room and linen closet exploded in here," Tommy said when they could see the other side.

It was true—there was a lot to navigate in the little hallway. Finally, after another several minutes, they made it to the bathroom.

Gem's tail thumped at the sight of Laurel. "Good dog, Gem!" Laurel patted her leg and Gem moved to her side while Erik knelt to check the girl's pulse. It was there . . . barely.

"She's cold, and her breathing is shallow," he said. Laurel saw the two medics exchange a concerned look. They knew what this meant; time was of the essence. They sprang into action. "Laurel, go grab some of those towels so we can cover her while we wait for help."

Laurel did as she was told, choosing the driest and cleanest linens she could find. When she returned with an armful of once-yellow towels, Erik and Tommy were discussing ways to get the girl out. It was clear that they didn't have the time it took to get *in*, so they had to come up with an alternative plan . . . something faster.

Erik radioed out to the larger team, letting them know where they were located in the house and what the conditions were.

Laurel spotted a crack in the skewed roof. "Do you think they could get an excavator to pull off the roof?" she asked. "We could use the bathtub to protect her . . ."

Tommy nodded. "That's what we were thinking, too. It's risky, but there aren't a lot of other options."

Erik finished his conversation and holstered the radio. "They agree. Pulling off the roof is the best chance we—I mean she—has. If we can do that, we can helicopter her out from here." He let out a slow breath. "They should be ready to go in about five minutes."

35

It took all three of the rescuers to drag the heavy tub a few inches closer to the wall in order to protect the unconscious girl as much as possible.

"I think that's the best we can do," Erik said as they huffed. "We've got to take cover in the hall." He waved his hand toward the spot he thought offered the best shelter during the roof demolition. They could hear the rumble of the excavator approaching as they scrambled into the corridor. Gem lagged behind, whimpering and unwilling to stray from the human she'd found.

"Come on, Gem," Laurel called, patting her leg.

Gem looked back at her handler, her eyes more liquid than usual. She really didn't want to come. She wanted to stay with the girl. The girl was in trouble. The girl needed her.

"All right, stay," Laurel said as Gem curled up tightly beneath the lip of the tub beside the teen.

"It's cast iron under that porcelain if that makes you feel any better," Tommy offered reassuringly. "Sturdy as all get-out. They're safer than we are."

The three workers hunkered down beside the cleaning closet as the roar of the giant machine rumbled closer. The house shuddered for several long seconds, and the sound of giant metal teeth clamping around the eave of the roof split their ears. Laurel closed her eyes as the shaking increased and then stopped for a moment. All at once everything lurched upward. Light flooded over them, and Laurel shielded her now-open eyes. The roof over their heads was gone!

"Holy moly!" Laurel exclaimed as she got to her

feet and waded to the bathroom door. Gem was still there, curled up beside the girl. Both were safe.

"No kidding," Tommy agreed.

They could hear several rescue workers outside now, shouting communications and excitement, then the thunderous sound of the medevac helicopter. A stretcher was lowered into the bathroom, and Erik and Tommy used a piece of wood to keep the girl's body in position as they gently lifted her onto it and strapped her in. An oxygen mask was fitted onto her face, and as the stretcher began to rise, they saw her eyelids flutter.

Erik beamed at Tommy, and then Laurel. "That's a good sign," he said. "A *very* good sign."

With the victim evacuated and on her way to the hospital, it was time for the crew to make its way out, too. Gem led them down the hall, patiently waiting while they climbed over mess and waded through the mud. The cherry picker was still waiting next to the boulder in the living room. It was an even tighter squeeze with Gem on board, but they managed to fit.

Outside, Erik and Tommy turned their attention to Gem, the hero of the day. "You are one incredible dog," Erik said while Tommy ruffled her mud-covered scruff.

Laurel beamed as Gem lapped up the attention. She was grateful that Gem was okay, that they had done some real good.

"I have to go check on my crew," Erik said. "And I'll see if I can get some info on the girl. Sometimes they let us know quickly if there's an ID or an update—especially with kids."

"I'd love to hear whatever you find out," Laurel replied.

Tommy gave Gem one last pet, then picked up his pole and went back to probing the mud.

Alone with her prized pup, Laurel gave Gem some much-deserved praise, water, and treats from the bag in her pocket. "You really, truly, are my wonder dog," she whispered. "One hundred percent."

Before long Erik was back with the report that the girl had been identified when she arrived at the hospital. Her name was Casey Jorgen. "Finding her was a miracle," he said, shaking his head in happy disbelief.

Laurel let the information sink in for a minute. Dozens of people were still missing in the mud, but Casey Jorgen had been found, alive. Found by Gem. "*You* are the miracle," she whispered.

When she lifted her face from Gem's neck, she saw a man stumbling toward them. It took her a moment to realize it was the man they'd met at the beginning of the day—the man in shock who'd said his family was just . . . gone. It seemed like so long ago, yet it had only been a matter of hours.

"You found my Casey," he blurted as he nearly collapsed next to them. "That was my Casey." His face was covered in muddy streaks, and his body shook with emotion and shock and fatigue. "She's not out of the woods yet, but if you hadn't found her there . . ." He shuddered again, his shoulders shaking. "Just . . . thank you."

Gem leaned toward the sobbing man and licked his cheek, which brought on another round of tears. Laurel gripped his arm and felt her own heart squeeze. "You're welcome" was all she could say.

36

After dinner on Thursday, the Sterling family gathered around the television as they had been ordered to by the littlest thing on two legs at the ranch: Juniper.

Georgia and Martin's youngest daughter stood in front of the screen holding the remote over her head and looking like an impatient tour guide at a museum.

"Uhhhh-uhhm." She cleared her throat.

Morgan nudged Forrest. Forrest nudged her back too hard with his elbow. Morgan fell into Shelby, who shoved her off and gave her "that look."

"Uhhh-uhhm!" Juniper cleared her throat again, and the crowd finally settled. Her parents were looking far too amused, and her siblings were not paying near enough attention. Only her grandmother, Frances, and her Lab, Cocoa, seemed to be taking this with the appropriate level of seriousness. They sat still in their seats and gave Juniper their undivided attention.

"Ladies and gentlemen, canines and felines!" Juniper included her cats even though they were nowhere in sight. "It is no secret to all of us here that Twig and Bud are the smartest, most adorable, most talented animals alive." She glanced at Cocoa apologetically, and Frances pretended to cover the brown dog's ears so she wouldn't be insulted.

"Soon, the secret will be out in the world . . ." Juniper paused dramatically and stepped to the side of the screen. I present to you, Bud Sequoia Cheshire Sterling in his world-premiere debut!" She pressed play.

Forrest nudged Morgan again, but both of them

kept their eyes glued to the screen as Bud strolled into the frame, sauntering serenely at cat's-eye level. Looking properly aloof, he crossed a pristine kitchen to a large, waiting bowl filled with colorful kibble.

The crowd went wild.

Juniper shushed them.

Bud proceeded to chew and crunch the kibble, and after a few close-up mouthfuls, the camera zoomed out so he could weave in and out of a pair of legs while producing his trademark engine-rumble purr.

"Meow Chow. They'll love you for it!" the voice-over announced as a tagline appeared on the bottom of the screen, complete with a heart-shaped paw print.

Everyone clapped, and Juniper, who had at last managed to lure Bud into the room during the first ever screening of his television debut, grabbed the star and took a bow along with him while Twig trotted past, unmoved.

"Great job, Bud." Morgan jumped up to give the champion purrer a pet.

Juniper nodded. "He really did nail it," she agreed. "Maybe now we can get a *new* agent." She rolled her eyes and released her grip on Bud, who promptly retreated to the corner to lick himself.

"Hopefully this new agent will help you get paid in cash?" her dad suggested lightly. "I don't know where I'm going to store all that cat food on a dog ranch."

"Bud and Twig don't even like it!" Juniper crowed. "They had to put tuna juice on top to get Bud to eat it during filming!"

Georgia giggled and covered her mouth. She knew better than to laugh at Juniper . . . or her husband. She was about to suggest they donate a substantial amount of Meow Chow to the local shelter, when her phone rang. It was a FaceTime call from a number she recognized. Pushing a few buttons, she mirrored her screen with the TV monitor and accepted the call. A familiar face replaced the number.

"Laurel! Good to see you! You caught us all together!"

Laurel's eyes grew wide, and she waved with the hand that was not holding the phone. "Hi, everyone!" She sounded excited, and her smile was wide.

The Sterlings shouted back their greetings, drowning one another out until Juniper climbed onto a chair.

"Shhhh! Everybody!" She hushed the room to be sure she was hearing what she thought she was hearing: familiar barks! "Gem! It's Gem! Say hi, Bud!"

Laurel laughed, bringing her dog into the frame on the call so they could see her for a second. She had to rein in the conversation, or leash it, or something . . .

"I called because I have big news," Laurel said. "Did you hear about the awful mudslides in Southern California?"

Georgia covered her mouth again. Of course she had heard. They all had. She kept her mouth covered while Laurel told the story of Gem's first rescue. By the time Laurel finished, there were tears in Georgia's eyes. Laurel had to swallow hard, too.

"Gem got in there. I thought the house was going to come the rest of the way down on her at any second, on all of us! But she dug her way through to find the girl, and we got Casey out just in time. We even visited her in the hospital. She's going to make a full recovery, thanks to Gem."

Georgia gulped. She had read about the teenager rescued from the big slides. It stuck with her because Casey was the same age as her Shelby. She sprang to her feet and wrapped her kids—all of them—in a hug. Juniper was first to wriggle free.

"Gem did it!" Juniper shouted as she danced around the living room. "I *knew* she was a rescue dog!" She suddenly stopped dancing and popped her fists onto her hips. Her eyebrows went up and her lips puckered into a bow. "And being a digger turned out to be a good thing after all," she said in her best "I told you so" voice. She shook her head, annoyed by the stupidity of human beings and their constant underestimation of animals.

"It sure did, Juniper!" Laurel, who was still on-screen, agreed, crouching down to wrap her arms around her best dog. "Our little digger is a rescue gem!"

A NOTE FROM THE AUTHORS

As bona fide dog lovers we jumped at the opportunity to write stories about rescue dogs. Knowing that the project would require extensive research, we excitedly explored websites, books, articles, and anything else that could help us learn about rescue dog training, handler pairing, and the disasters dogs assist with. We found dozens of inspiring stories about real dogs doing what they do best: acting selflessly, loyally, enthusiastically, tirelessly, and heroically to save people in peril. We were won over by these incredible tales of canines and their companions, and inspired by the dedication and hard work so many two- and four-legged creatures undertake in service of others. We also learned that there are many differing theories and methods of dog training.

It can take years of training and discipline to develop dogs' natural gifts into skills that make them both safe and effective helpers in the aftermath of disasters. Dozens of canine search and rescue agencies all over the world do this important work, and while they all share the common goal of creating well-matched and successful dog-and-handler teams, each has its own philosophy and style. There is no single path to becoming a certified search dog. Though we were particularly inspired by the National Disaster Search Dog Foundation, established by Wilma Melville and her Labrador, Murphy, we pulled from several schools of thought regarding both training and searching to create these dog-inspired fictional stories. We hope you enjoy them. Woof!

ABOUT THE AUTHORS

Jane B. Mason and Sarah Hines Stephens are co-authors of several middle-grade novels, including the A Dog and His Girl Mysteries series and the Candy Apple titles *The Sister Switch* and *Snowfall Surprise*. As Sarah Jane they wrote the critically acclaimed *Maiden Voyage: A Titanic Story*. *Ember, Dusty,* and *Jet* are the first three books in their Rescue Dogs series.